THE EXECUTIVE

WINTER RENSHAW

EXMAS

Winter Renshaw
© 2018

COPYRIGHT

IMPORTANT!

Let me first say: Reed York was never my boyfriend. He was
the pen. I was the company ink. Though if you want to get
technical, we were more like colleagues-who-hated-each-
other ... with benefits.

Everything was fine until the charming jerk went behind
my back, stole my promotion, and became my boss—literally
overnight.

Refusing to work beneath him (professionally speaking and
otherwise), I transferred 2,014 miles away to our Chicago
division, and I've spent the past year trying to remember
how much I hated his panty-melting smirk so I can forget
how much I secretly loved the way his ocean eyes lit every
time I walked into the room.

But he's just announced a last-minute site visit next week,

and on top of that, he's audaciously designated me as his 'right hand gal' during his visit. If he thinks he has a snowball's chance in this hell at getting back in my good graces, he's got another thing coming.

Reed York might be a man used to getting everything he's ever wanted, but Joa Jolivet is a woman that never forgets.

PLAYLIST

Holly Jolly Christmas – Michael Bublé
White Christmas – Bring Crosby
Have Yourself a Merry Little Christmas – Frank Sinatra
Jingle Bells – Duke Ellington
Caroling, Caroling – Nat King Cole
Merry Christmas, Baby – Otis Redding
Let it Snow! Let it Snow! Let it Snow! – Frank Sinatra
All I Want for Christmas is You – Michael Bublé
I've Got My Love to Keep Me Warm – Dean Martin
What Are You Doing New Year's Eve – Ella Fitzgerald

For Louisa Maggio.

AUTHOR'S NOTE

Dear Reader,

Interspersed between the chapters of this book are short flashback vignettes that tie into the present-day chapter that preceded it. The vignettes are not dated, nor are they in chronological order, they're simply relevant to that particular part of the story. Also, if you aren't into flashbacks, you can skip them. The present-day story unfolds the same either way (though I highly recommend not skipping them so that you're able to experience the full depth of Reed and Joa's story).

Enjoy!

Winter xx

Love me. I'm cold.
—Atticus

Joa

To say it's the most wonderful time of the year would be an understatement. Though if you'd have asked me a year ago, I'd have vehemently disagreed.

Last Christmas was a nightmare of epic proportions, but fortunately the sole asshole responsible for that hot mess is light years away.

Two thousand and fourteen miles away, to be exact.

He couldn't ruin my holidays if he tried.

"You wanted to see me?" I stand in the doorway of my boss' office Friday afternoon and check my watch. I was supposed to leave after lunch today, but he sent an email asking me to meet him at one o'clock for a quick chat. He ended his email with his signature smiley-face, so I'm not worried, but it doesn't make me any less annoyed at the fact that I should be at home right now, peeling out of this pantsuit and kicking off these toe-pinching heels as I fix myself a Hot Toddy and watch *The Family Stone* for the fifth time this month.

"Shut the door, please, Joa, will you?" Smiley-face Harold folds his hands across his desk, waiting.

"Is everything okay?" I take a seat in the chair across from him. "You're making me nervous. Is this about the Gilliam account? Because I heard from Julie, and they're signing first thing after the New Year."

"No, no." Harold flashes a tender smile that dissipates a moment later. "Corporate is coming next week."

I wrinkle my nose. "Corporate? Why?"

Harold shrugs. "Your guess is as good as mine. But they're sending the CFO."

My stomach turns. "What? Why?"

"I don't know, Joa. This is news to me too." Harold's liver-spotted forehead creases and he reaches for a pen, tapping it on his desk and twirling it between his fingers. In the year that I've worked under this man, I've yet to see him break a sweat over anything, but he can't sit still to save his life right now.

"Are you familiar with Mr. York? From your time at the LA branch?" he asks, referring to the current CFO of Genesis Financial Securities. Turns out the position he stole from me a year ago was nothing more than a stepping stone for him, a mere rung on a ladder. He wasn't Vice President of Acquisitions more than four months before he was tapped for the CFO spot.

Must be hard getting everything you've ever wanted with the flash of your brilliant white smile …

No one ever said life was fair, but news of his promotion was a kick in the teeth that I remedied with an entire bottle of Pinot Noir and a two-hour rant session to my Chi-Town work bestie, Lucy Clarke.

"I … know *of* him. Why do you ask?" I answer his question with one of my own.

Harold places the pen flat on his desk and folds his hands before leaning forward. "He's asked for your assistance during his tenure here."

I snort. "I'd be happy to recommend a concierge service. Chicago is full of them. And tenure? What do you mean tenure? How long is he planning to stay?"

Harold blows a breath through pursed lips and shakes his head. "I don't know. His email said it would be the week leading up to Christmas and possibly through New Year's, with an extension if necessary."

"This is a really busy time for me ..." I say, hoping he doesn't call my bluff and pull up my calendar. Last I looked I had all of three standing appointments between now and January fourth.

Harold offers an apologetic half wince. "Joa... he asked for you personally. He wants you to be his right-hand gal, so to speak. He's my boss. He's your boss, too, if we want to get technical. We're not in any kind of position to tell him no."

I choke on my spit when I try to respond, and then the words get lost.

"Firstly," I manage to say, "I'm an acquisitions coordinator for the Chicago territory. I'm not a coffee runner or reservation maker or dry cleaner picker upper."

Harold places his hand out, maybe to stop me, maybe to imply that he understands, but I go on.

"I'm sorry, Harold. I've always done what you've asked me to do, but I can't do this."

He frowns, an unusual expression for Smiley Face Harold. "I'm sorry. My hands are tied on this."

"Then I'll tell him 'no' myself." I rise from my chair, my feet aching, my dress nearly strangling the air from my lungs.

Harold examines me, probably wondering what this is

about. And I don't blame him. I never told him why I transferred from LA to Chicago, and he never asked. He's always been hands-off like that, a trait I've grown to appreciate. And he's always gone to bat for his staff. But he's powerless as far as Reed's absurd request goes, so I'll have to deal with him myself.

A year of trying to forget his cedar and vetiver cologne and the way that gaze of his lit like a struck match every time I walked into the room, a year of deleting his bullshit company-wide emails and purposely scheduling client meetings and lunches during branch-wide conference calls so I didn't have to hear the velvet tenor of his voice ... only to be forced to endure his presence in the very refuge I sought to escape him – is the very definition of unfair.

"Joa ..." Harold stands, tugging on the hem of his suit jacket. "I would heavily advise against that."

"All right. I'm off." I walk to the door, ignoring his unsolicited advice. "See you Monday."

Slinging my bag over my shoulder, I make it all the way to the elevator before the reality of the situation turns my legs to gelatin and sucks the Christmas-scented air from my lungs.

I don't know why he's coming or what he wants, but if it's me – he's wasting his very expensive, CFO-salaried time.

A blink later, I'm adjusting my knit hat and dashing through the slushy Chicago sidewalks to catch the L to quaint, suburban Mills Haven, where I reside in a charming brick brownstone half a mile from my childhood home, four blocks from my sister and her family, a half hour from my brother in Wicker Park, and a world away from my life back in LA—which is equal parts bittersweet and promising.

Giant snowflakes melt on my face as I pass carolers and

bell ringers. Digging into the bottom of my bag, I grab a handful of change and deposit it into a red kettle before locating my Ventra pass.

The past year has been an adjustment, but in the best of ways. I've found my footing back home—which is crazy because all I ever wanted to do growing up was live anywhere but here.

The Chicago team is smaller than the LA team. More family-like. More personable. Much less drama. There are eleven of us—and I know everyone's spouses' names, whether or not they have pets, and how they take their coffee or if they prefer tea, if they're on some kind of Intermittent Fasting Keto diet this week or if they recently discovered the evils of gluten.

My place in Mills Haven is a little cheaper and a little bigger than my apartment in LA was. And I've spent every major holiday plus every Sunday dinner at my parents' house, which I'll admit is a lot more enjoyable when I'm not on the other side of a computer screen partaking via Skype. I've caught up with old friends from high school. Dated a couple of nice-as-pie average Joes who were a tall drink of the most refreshing water compared to Reed, and next year, I've decided to get a dog.

Life is good.

And once I get through these next couple of weeks, it'll be even better.

This is just a minor hiccup, an annoyance. That's all. Like a rash you have to ignore until it clears up.

I refuse to let him ruin another Christmas.

PAST

Joa

"Everyone, I'd like you to meet Joa Jolivet." *Genesis Financial Securities president and founder Elliot Grosvenor introduces me in front of no less than twenty-five staffers, but in a sea of unfamiliar faces, a striking set of diamond-blue eyes catch my attention.*

With hair the color of Pacific coast sand, a stone gray suit that strains against his shoulders, and a panty-melting smirk on his full lips, I make a mental note to steer clear of that one.

There's heartbreak written all over him.

"Joa brings with her a masters' degree in business administration from Purdue University with a focus on finance," *Elliot continues. A girl in a white blouse yawns and checks her manicure. A guy next to her checks his Apple watch.* *"Her thesis was on the effect of cryptocurrency on the private financial sector. Quite an impressive read. Highly recommend checking it out if you haven't yet. Anyway, Joa, we're*

thrilled to have you here, and I have no doubt you'll fit right in."

"Thank you, Elliot," I say from my seat. "Excited to be here."

God, I sound like a dweeb, but honestly, I couldn't care less. I've just landed my dream job working in the budding cryptocurrency industry. Nothing else really matters.

Diamond Eyes is still staring at me, his thumb sliding up and down his silver pen.

My attention diverts to Grosvenor as he mentions a couple of bullet point items and dismisses us a moment later.

The team files out and a couple of people stop and introduce themselves, but Diamond Eyes takes his sweet time.

I imagine he's the kind of guy who always gets what he wants with the flash of his perfect smile. Unfortunately for him, I won't be had that easily.

I didn't come here to date.

And I don't do the whole pen-and-company-ink thing.

The SoCal Adonis in the gray suit makes his way over, laser-focused, and I swallow the lump in my throat and straighten my shoulders.

"Reed York," he says with guarded authority. "You're on my team."

"There are four of us, right?" I ask.

"Right."

"And we all do the same thing?"

His sparkling gaze squints. "Right."

"So it's not technically ... your ... team," I say.

"Semantics." He studies me for a minute before shaking his head and wiping the smirk off his distractingly kissable mouth. "You're going to keep me on my toes. I can already tell."

"Meaning is everything," I say. "I minored in communications."

"Yeah, well, I'm more of a numbers guy," he says. "Anyway, Phillips tasked me with training you, so ... lucky you."

He flashes a smile that sends an electric zing to my core.

As long as he keeps his pen from my ink, we should have nothing to worry about.

REED

"VISITING FAMILY?"

I glance up to my First-Class seatmate, a sixty-something woman with silvery hair, diamond studs in her ears, and a lavender cashmere twinset.

"Chicago at Christmastime is just lovely," she adds. "My daughter and son-in-law live there. He's a pediatric surgeon. One of the best in the state. They're expecting their third baby any day now, so I haven't booked my return flight yet. Fingers crossed we have a little one to hold before the new year."

The cabin doors have been secured and the flight attendant passes through the aisle, and I take a quick look around, hoping to eye an empty seat so I can get away from Chatty Cathy, but no dice.

"Do you have any children?" she asks.

I bite the inside of my lip and look away before I make an ass of myself and ask this woman if she's never flown

First Class before. It'd be the only explanation as to why she's not following the first unspoken rule of this section of the cabin—mind your own business.

A chime interrupts her before she has a chance to start again, and the captain's voice fills the speakers. "Ladies and gentlemen, this is your captain speaking. Your flight attendants are preparing the cabin for takeoff. In just a few minutes, we're going to ..."

Chatty Cathy listens carefully, and I dig into my inner jacket pocket to find my ear pods—only one seems to have vanished.

Of course.

"Champagne?" A caramel-haired attendant stops at our row.

"Oh, my goodness. Yes, please!" Chatty Cathy says before leaning toward me. "I've never flown First Class before."

Was I right or was I right?

The attendant looks to me and I shake my head. Once we take off, I'll order my usual two fingers of whiskey, pop in my lone ear bud, and close my eyes.

"My daughter and son-in-law bought me this ticket," she continues. How she hasn't yet noticed the one-sidedness of this conversation is beyond me. "She wanted to surprise me with an upgrade. A little Christmas gift, I suppose. I'm sorry—you seem a little agitated. Are you one of those people who get scared on airplanes?"

I stifle a chuckle before giving her side eye. "No."

"You're just so ... quiet." She toys with the diamond cross pendant dangling from her neck, tapping her fake red nails against it as she studies me. "Me, I have the opposite problem. I get nervous when I fly and then I can't stop talking."

She laughs—no, cackles. The suited man across from us shoots her a look.

"Magazine? Newspaper?" A different attendant stops beside us. "Last chance before takeoff."

"Well, let's see. What do you have?" Chatty Cathy asks, clucking her tongue and perusing like we have all the time in the world. "Oh, I'll take this one. Thank you."

Finally.

Paging through a pristine issue of Good Housekeeping, the woman stops after a minute and folds it in her lap.

"I'm sorry—I just can't help noticing how agitated you are," she says to me. "Something is clearly bothering you, and you know how I can tell? I'm a body language expert. I've written three books on the subject. Your breathing and your rigid posture and the way you keep situating and re-situating yourself in these extremely comfortable chairs ... the fact that you refuse to engage in small talk ... It's the holidays, isn't it?"

I can't help but chuckle at her audacity and the blatant irony that lies in the fact that she can pick up on body language cues and brag about her expertise but be so socially inept.

"Name's Reed," I say, giving her my full attention now as we taxi to the runway. "And you're correct. I am agitated. But it has nothing to do with the holidays or flying."

"Reed. That's a lovely name. I'm Saundra," she says, a pleased gleam in her gray eyes. "With an 'a' and a 'u'."

"I'm actually traveling for work and I've got a lot on my plate, so if you don't mind ..." I offer the politest smile I can muster and lift my ear bud before placing it in my left ear.

"Traveling for work? Over *Christmas*? Your boss must be a real Scrooge."

I harbor a full breath in my lungs, resisting the urge to exhale loudly. "I'm my own boss."

I mean, technically the president of the company is a step above me, but he doesn't have the balls to fire me—not after the information that's recently come to light ... which is part of why I'm making this trip, but that's neither here nor there.

"*Oh.*" Saundra rests her manicured palm on top of the glossy magazine in her lap, brows meeting as she stares at the seatback in front of her.

Leaning toward the window, I close my eyes and offer a soundless prayer for silence to the merciful Gods of Holiday Airline Travel. Fortunately they hear my plea, because the moment we're in the air, I steal a quick peak at Saundra and find her passed out, mouth agape, a pink shawl wrapped around her shoulders.

Turns out, though, that it doesn't matter. Without Saundra's gums flapping in my ear, my own thoughts are just as loud and busy, just as focused as ever on the one thing that hasn't left my mind since the day she left LA: Joa Jolivet.

PAST

Reed

I check my watch, waiting for Grosvenor to shuffle in with the newest hire, some recent college graduate from the middle of nowhere. I'm sure she flew out here with Hollywood stars in her eyes and sky-high ambitions that'll be crushed by the time she finishes her first apartment lease.

I notice her from my peripheral vision first. Maybe it's the cherry red sweater that matches her full, glossed lips or the sleek onyx hair draped over her shoulder and tucked behind one ear. A string of pearls circles her neck. She's a vision of Old Hollywood glam mixed with a modern twist, and I can't take my fucking eyes off her.

I want.

No. I need ...

"Everyone, I'd like you to meet Joa Jolivet," Grosvenor introduces her, and she offers the sweetest, understated smile I've ever seen as her sapphire gaze scans the room, stopping on me.

"Joa brings with her a masters' degree in business administration from Purdue University with a focus on finance," Elliot continues. Deidra yawns and checks her chipped manicure. Maxwell checks his Apple watch for the twentieth time. "Her thesis was on the effect of cryptocurrency on the private financial sector. Quite an impressive read. Highly recommend checking it out if you haven't yet. Anyway, Joa, we're thrilled to have you here, and I have no doubt you'll fit right in."

"Thank you, Elliot," she says. "Excited to be here."

She sounds like a nerd, but if she's a nerd, she's the sexiest nerd I've ever seen in my entire life.

I haven't had the strength to look away yet, and my pen is gripped so tight in my hands I feel the metal bend and threaten to snap.

Grosvenor drones on with a couple of reminder items and tells us to get back to work.

The team files out and a couple of people stop and introduce themselves, but I take my time so I have a chance to introduce myself personally.

Making my way to her once the room has emptied, I watch her shoulders straighten and her lips press flat as she swallows.

"Reed York," I say. "You're on my team."

"There are four of us, right?" she asks.

"Right."

"And we all do the same thing?"

I squint. "Right."

"So it's not technically ... your ... team," she says.

Sassy. Outspoken. Brazen.

Hot as fuck.

"Semantics." I study her for a minute before shaking my head and hiding the smirk on my face with the brush of my hand. *"You're going to keep me on my toes. I can already tell."*

"Meaning is everything," she says. *"I minored in communications."*

"Yeah, well, I'm more of a numbers guy," I tell her. *"Anyway, Phillips tasked me with training you, so ... lucky you."*

I can't help but flash a smirk when I notice the way her chest rises and falls and her eyes shift on mine. I'm all but reading her thoughts at this point.

Call it a gut feeling, but I'm two hundred percent sure Joa Jolivet wants me.

And I'm two hundred percent okay with that.

Joa

"IF YOU NEED A BUFFER, I'm your girl," Lucy from work says through the speaker on my phone Friday night.

I'd never so much as mentioned Reed to her in the past. Never brought up our history. Never went into specifics about why I took the transfer. As soon as I stepped onto Illinois soil, nothing else mattered. I left the past in the past where it belonged. Besides, no one wants to draw attention to their bad decisions.

But tonight, she got an earful.

"That's sweet of you, Luc, but I don't need a buffer," I say, though the burgeoning pit in my stomach begs to differ. "I'm just going to be professional and cordial and ... and ... get through it."

"Sounds like a plan." I can almost see her rolling her eyes from behind her signature red frames.

The Family Stone is paused on my TV, my Hot Toddy is now nothing more than a Lukewarm Todd, and I haven't stopped pacing since I got home. I've even found myself grabbing random things just to touch them and then putting them back in the most random of places. Throw blanket on the bathroom counter? Remote in the fridge? And I can't stop checking my reflection, though I haven't the slightest clue what I'm looking for.

I'm hell bent on standing my ground with Reed come Monday, but I'm not sure how I'm going to do that if the mere mention of him coming to the city has me this frazzled and scattered. He's the only man in the history of men to make me act *and* feel like I'm losing my mind, and I hate him for that.

I stop pacing, but only long enough to check myself in the hall mirror for the billionth time. The woman staring back at me with her familiar onyx hair and hooded baby blue eyes looks equal parts terrified and ready for battle, and of course she does. The enemy is about to cross a line drawn in the sand somewhere around Edgewater, Colorado, where our physical halfway point lies and our work territories are divided.

"What do you think he wants anyway?" Lucy asks. "It's just so random that the CFO would plan a last-minute site visit right before the holidays. Do you think he's going to personally deliver our Christmas bonuses?"

"Ha. Right. You don't know him like I do."

"Obviously."

"He doesn't give two shits about anyone but himself. He couldn't be bothered to hop a flight across the country to personally deliver Christmas bonuses. Believe me, he's got better things to do with his time," I say.

"Then what could it be? Are they closing the branch?"

I thought about that on the ride home tonight but quickly ruled it out. "No way. We're having our best year yet. We're outperforming the East Coast with half as many clients. There's no way they're cutting us."

"Ah, true, true." Lucy exhales into the receiver. "Then that only leaves one other logical explanation."

"What's that?"

"He's coming because of *you*."

If I had a drink in my mouth, I'd spit it out. "Sorry, Luc, but that's the most ridiculous thing I've ever heard. He's well aware of the fact that I want nothing to do with him."

"Is he though? Have you ever actually told him that?"

"In not so many words, yes," I say. "Radio silence can be deafeningly loud in the right situations. Plus, we were nothing more than fuck buddies. LA is filled to the brim with beautiful women who would give their left breast implant for a chance to date this asshole. He's not going to hop on a plane and fly two thousand miles on the off chance he might be able to get a piece from an old co-worker."

"When you put it that way ... I guess." She pauses for a second. "It's just that, when you talk about him, you talk about him like he's your ex-boyfriend."

"I mean, yeah. We spent time together. We took trips— but only because hooking up in the office got old after a bit. It was nice to get away ... but we were never dating. He never met my family. I never met his. We never hung out with each other's friends. Never got together for any reason that didn't revolve around an orgasm or two ..." A cheap thrill zings down my spine and my thighs clench, but I force the excitement away.

"If he was just some meaningless friend-with-benefits type of thing, I don't think you'd be this worked up, you know?" Lucy asks. "Whether you dated or not, he's still an ex. Even if he's just an ex friend-with-benefits. The two of you have a history. And it might be a little more complicated than you're willing to admit. And you need to own that or you're never going to get through this."

I let her words soak in for a second, though I refuse to tell her she's right because she already knows and it's going to make her already big head even bigger. I can't be responsible for Lucy Clarke's head exploding just a few days before Christmas.

"Own it, Joa," she says. "Hell, give it a silly name so we can laugh about it. Call the next couple of weeks Exmas or something. You'll get through this, but only with a sense of humor and a lot of self-reflection."

"God, you sound so much like your mother right now, it's unreal," I say, referring to world-renowned psychologist and syndicated talk show host, Dr. Candice Clarke.

"*Anyway.*" The sound of microwave buttons beeping fills the background of her side of the call. "I'm heating up my Lean Cuisine, and then I'm painting the town with a few girls from spin class. Sure you don't want to tag along?"

"Nah. I'm staying in. I'm watching my nieces in the morning so my sister can wrap presents, and I promised I'd bring them sticky rolls, so I'm going to call it a night in a couple of hours."

"Lame."

"Have a drink for me," I say, eyeing my Lukewarm Todd, which can probably be further downgraded to a Cool T by now. "See you Monday."

"Yeah, yeah." She hangs up and I dock my phone on a nearby charger.

Sarah Jessica Parker's face fills the paused TV screen in my living room—her hair slicked back tight and hands clasped nervously in front of her hips as she meets Dermot Mulroney's family for the first time. While I can't relate to her character, I can't help but love this movie. It's not exactly a Christmas classic, but it isn't a holiday season if I don't watch it at least a handful of times. If Lucy were inside my head right now, she'd probably be analyzing my love for this storyline, saying it represents family and togetherness—which are of utmost importance to me— but also that it represents knowing what you *want* and then discovering what you *need* instead.

Meredith *wanted* Everett. But he was all wrong for her. She *needed* Ben. He made her a better person. He brought out her best qualities while Everett enabled her worst ones.

Do we ever truly know what we need though until we're gobsmacked upside the head with it? Seems like that's always how it works. It's always easier, I think, to figure out what we don't need.

I don't need Reed York. I know that.

Life's a hell of a lot simpler without him wading in my waters, mucking everything up, but the mire should settle as soon as he leaves, and life as I know it will continue on.

I hit the play button on the remote, and SJP's expression unfreezes as she goes in for an awkward hug as she meets her boyfriend's mother for the first time.

Rivulets of melting snow glide down my living room window, and outside a car pulls into the driveway I share with my next-door neighbor, Mrs. Kellerman. A family of five piles out a second later, grabbing wrapped presents and various-sized suitcases from the trunk, and it brings a smile to my face. Maybe it's a good thing he's coming to town over the holidays. Maybe when I'm not at work, I'll be so busy and distracted by family gatherings and holiday parties and last-minute Christmas shopping and baking to even remember he's here.

I microwave my drink before settling in again, trying like hell to keep sharp, focused.

I can do this.

I've got a full weekend to harden my resolve, to prepare myself for Monday morning.

Reed York might be a man used to getting everything he's ever wanted, but Joa Jolivet is a woman who never forgets.

He might want me, but he's not getting me.

Everyone knows naughty boys only get coal for Christmas.

PAST

Joa

Zippers. His and mine.

Breathless sighs. His and mine.

Wild eyes. His and mine.

Held tongues. His and mine.

"This can't happen again." I break the silence and smooth my hands over my skirt and put my desk back together. "I don't get involved with people I work with."

Reed straightens his tie. "Sure, Joa. Whatever you say."

An hour ago we were poring over spreadsheets, sharing my computer monitor. He kept reaching over me, his arm brushing mine, his intoxicating cologne invading my space like he owned it.

Every time he leaned in a little closer, my heart sped a little faster.

There's no denying he's unfairly attractive. Tall. Runner's body. Chiseled jaw. Blue eyes that damn near shimmer when he looks my way.

And the way he struts around the office, so confident, so sure of himself. It both irritates and turns me on—and always at the same time.

I've only been here three weeks, and already he's sparked not one but two arguments with me in front of the entire team at our weekly sit-down meeting.

I'm not sure if my intelligence intimidates him or if he's trying to impress me with his own. Either way, if I spend more than an hour with him, I find myself wanting to slap the smirk off his face and wondering what it'd be like to kiss his full lips.

Tonight, I got my answer.

But it can't happen again.

And it won't.

4

REED

I PUNCH the six-digit code into the lock at the apartment I AirBnB'd for my trip. The code box beeps a second later and the lock releases with a metallic clunk. I could've rented a suite at the Four Seasons, but there's something sad and depressing about staying in a hotel—alone—over the holidays. Plus, this place is two blocks from the office.

Pushing the door open, I roll my luggage in and let it shut behind me before getting the lights.

The couple who own the place are spending the month in Istanbul, visiting family for the holidays, so why the hell they'd decorate the place for Christmas is beyond me, but sure enough, there are garlands and silver tinsel and faux trees and chunky knit stockings and little ceramic snowman figurines shoved and crammed in every corner of this place —so *not* what was pictured.

"Nice." I groan, unloading my pockets onto the kitchen

counter. Billfold. Keys from home, because I feel naked without them. Phone. Some loose change.

I'm quite certain that under all this holiday cheer is a pretty decent place, though it's hard to appreciate all the marble and hardwood and high-end furnishings with all this green and red elf vomit clouding up the view.

I take a look around, familiarizing myself with the layout, before unpacking my things in the bedroom. The owners have cleared out a few drawers and half a closet for my stay, and the bathroom is spotless, so there's that.

Kicking my shoes off, I make myself comfortable on their four-poster king-sized bed and reach for the remote. Scanning the listings, I find nothing but shitty Christmas movies and bad reality show re-runs. If I were back in LA, I'd be meeting up for drinks with friends or trying to hit some golf balls while there's still daylight, but it's late here now. And dark. And I don't know a single person in the area besides the one who wants nothing to do with me, so ... *Christmas Vacation* it is.

My phone chimes with a text from my younger sister, Bijou, asking what the plans are for Christmas this year. The last eight years, my parents have booked solo trips to places like Tahiti and the Maldives or St. Croix, leaving the two of us to fend for ourselves—which is fine. We're grown adults pushing thirty, but somehow that's morphed into my sister expecting me to make plans for the two of us, and if I'm being honest, Christmas is just another day to me.

New Year's Eve though, that's my night.

Expensive drinks, a beautiful girl to kiss at midnight, and a party so big it spans the entire world.

I rub my heavy eyes and read her message again before deciding to call her. She answers in the middle of the second ring before converting the call to FaceTime.

"*Reeeeeed,*" she says, adjusting her phone on some kind of stand. Her face is covered in some avocado-looking face-mask and I almost want to tell her she looks like The Grinch when she smiles, her big, white teeth contrasting against the bright, garish green. "You get my text?"

"Obviously. That's why I'm calling."

She rolls her eyes. "Anyway. What's the plan for Thursday? Should we do brunch somewhere?"

That's become our tradition the last few years. Brunch and a matinee. Like we're some old married couple and not a brother and sister who grew up with all the advantages life had to offer except for a true sense of family togetherness.

If it was free, it was never of any value to Redford and Bebe York.

"I'm in Chicago," I say.

Bijou blinks. "What? Chicago? Why?"

"Work."

"Your boss made you travel over the holidays? What kind of—"

"Bij, I am the boss," I say. "I needed to take care of a few things that came up this past week. They couldn't wait. I'm sorry. Raincheck?"

Her nose wrinkles through her drying, flaking mask. "You can't *raincheck Christmas*. Who does that? Maybe I can come out there and see you?"

"I don't think that's a good idea."

"What, are you spending the holidays with someone special?" she asks in a teasing, kid-sister tone. "I didn't think you were dating anyone."

"No. And I'm not."

"Then why are you forcing me to spend Christmas Day alone like a loser?" she asks. "Mom and Dad are in freaking Fiji right now, soaking up the sun and swimming in clear water, and you're in some Winter Wonderland, and I'm just supposed to sit back here in LA and not care about the fact that everyone forgot about me this year?"

"No one forgot about you," I say with a chuckle. Growing up, Bijou put the Drama in Drama Queen and even at twenty-six, she's yet to shed that title.

"I'm going to have to stay in that day," she says. "Like a shut-in."

"Order some takeout. Watch some movies. Hell, read a damn book for once. You'll be fine."

"Can we at least FaceTime that day?" she asks.

"Yeah, sure."

"Good." Bijou smiles, making the mask around her mouth flake. "Ugh. I need to wash this off. It's starting to itch. Anyway, what are you going to do that day? You never said."

I shrug. "Haven't given it much thought."

The movie on the TV goes to commercial, and I climb off the bed. Not feeling the Griswold's tonight and I need to unpack anyway, so I might as well.

"Would you kill me if I just ... showed up in Chicago that day?" Bijou carries her phone to the bathroom, and the sound of running water fills the background.

"Yes."

Her smile fades. "Seriously, Reed, why are you acting like you're on some secret mission or something? Stop being weird."

"I'm tired," I lie. Kind of. "Been traveling all day. I need to unpack. Order some pizza."

"See. You *are* being weird. The Reed I know wouldn't stay in on a Friday night."

"I'll FaceTime you Thursday, all right?" I ask before ending the call.

"You really suck, you know that?" she asks. If I know my sister, and I do, she's going to hold this against me for the rest of our lives, just like she's never let me forget about the time I chased her with a Super Soaker filled with hot tap water on a ninety-degree day. "Love you, jerk face."

"Same." I hang up and retrieve my suitcase from the entryway, wheeling it back to the bedroom and working the lock on the zipper.

Though I'd hardly call myself nostalgic and I tend to leave the past in the past, I was strategic in my packing for this trip.

The mint green tie I wore the first time I had sex with Joa after a late night in the office.

The Creed Pure White cologne I used to wear that drove her wild and made it impossible for her to keep her hands off me.

The Burberry watch she picked out for me during one of our "sex-cations" in Saint Thomas.

Come Monday morning when I strut into the Chicago office, I'm going to be a walking, talking blast from the past, and I can't fucking wait to see the look on her face when she sees me.

I chuckle to myself as I hang up my navy suit. I bet she's wracking her brain, trying to figure out why I'd come all the way out here on such short notice. And knowing the class act that she is, I'm sure she intends to be professional and keep her distance and pretend like we didn't have sex seven times in one weekend in Napa two Septembers ago.

But I can't pretend. Couldn't if I tried. Truth be told, she's all I've thought about since the moment she walked out of the LA office and never came back.

As much as I've wanted to write her off, as much as I've spent the past year convincing myself she was nothing but a fuck buddy who meant nothing to me, I can't any longer. If she meant nothing to me, I wouldn't be so hung up on her after all this time. Pining for the one thing I can't have, the one thing I never knew I wanted until it was too late.

I know why she left.

I know what she thinks of me.

I know what I did and how it looks.

But she doesn't know the truth. And quite frankly, I'm not in a position to share that with her ... *yet*.

If I close my eyes, I can picture her crystalline baby blues and feel the silky soft waves of her dark-as-midnight hair in my hands. I can almost smell the sugar-sweet softness of her skin, can almost taste the honey musk of her arousal on my tongue.

But it's her voice I miss the most. The Liv Tyler-esque way she'd speak. Her words slow and intentional when we'd talk, like she had all the time in the world and I was the only person worthy of her undivided attention. No one else mattered. The outside world? Non-existent. And she could bring the most intense blanket of calmness to the most chaotic of days.

In the year that's passed, I've yet to meet another human being like Joa Jolivet. But that's okay because I refuse to settle for cheap knockoffs when only the original will do.

I hang the last of my suits in the closet before grabbing the final item from my luggage: a silver wrapped box tied with a blue satin bow—the one she'd tossed in the trash last December, unopened.

If all goes as planned this week, if I can get her to understand ... then maybe she'll finally get a chance to see what's inside. And if she likes it?

It'll change everything.

PAST

Reed

The first time is never the last time—at least not in my experience.

They always come back for more.

Joa buttons her blouse, standing before my office window, backlit by the lights of downtown LA and a moonlit sky.

Her dark hair covers her pale blue eyes and she dresses like she's got somewhere else to be.

"It's the fifth time in two weeks," I say.

"And your point?" She looks up, tucking a strand of hair behind her ear.

"If this is going to be a regular occurrence, we need to set some ground rules."

"Like?"

"This thing we're doing, it's monogamous," I say. "But we're not dating. We're not a couple."

"Good, because we'd probably murder each other before

our first anniversary." She sniffs, searching my office floor for her heels.

"No selfies. That's boyfriend/girlfriend territory. And apartments are off-limits. You don't come to mine, I don't come to yours."

"Okay. Can I ask why?"

"Just ... trust me. If this little arrangement is going to work, it's just the way it has to be. You start hanging out at each other's places and next thing you know, the lines begin to blur and you have to cut and run before it turns into a full-blown relationship."

"Sounds like you speak from experience."

"I just want this to work." I swipe one of her heels off the top of my desk, handing it to her. "Don't you?"

"So are we only ever going to hook up here? In the office?" She ignores my question in favor of one of her own. "I mean, if our places are off-limits, this whole thing could get stale quick."

I chuff. "Joa, I promise, nothing about this will ever be stale. And I'm more than happy to find us some other options —just no hotels."

Her nose wrinkles. "Why not?"

"I have my reasons."

"I'm sure we could find something nice."

"No," I say. "That's a hard limit."

"Hotels are a hard limit for you?" Her arms fold across her chest and her head cocks as she studies me. I bet she thinks I'm teasing. "For real, Reed?"

I check my watch. It's almost nine o'clock. Seems like lately we've been finding every excuse to stay late and bury ourselves in one of our offices until the place is empty and the cleaning crew has long gone home.

"Maybe we can mix it up a little," I say. "Once a month, we can take a trip somewhere for a long weekend."

Joa nods. "It'd be a way burn off some of this OT we've been racking up."

"I have credit card miles. We could go anywhere you want."

"That sounds like boyfriend/girlfriend territory."

"Not if we're careful."

5

Joa

"AUNT JOA, can we watch another movie?" My six-year-old niece, Emmeline, clasps her hands together, a fleece Minnie Mouse blanket covering her lap and remnants of this morning's sticky rolls on her rosy cheeks.

"Can we, can we?" her twin sister, Ellison, joins along, her big blue eyes as wide as they are round.

I know my sister and brother-in-law have strict screen time rules in their house, but he's at work and she's wrapping gifts at our parents' house and I'm in charge, so ...

"Sure, why not?" I grab the remote off the coffee table and navigate through Netflix until we get to some Angelina Ballerina movie and they tell me to stop.

"You're the best aunt in the whole world!" Emmeline wraps her arms around my neck.

"Except that one time when you made us go to bed early," Ellison says, crossing her arms and pouting her lower lip.

"It was Daylight Saving Time," I say.

"It was still light out," she says.

"Watch your rat movie," I tease, reaching across Emmeline and roughing Ellison's wild blonde mane.

"She's a mouse!" they both yell.

"My bad." I lift my palms in the air, pretending to surrender, and then I head to the kitchen to pour another cup of coffee.

I couldn't get comfortable last night, couldn't stop tossing and turning. And my mind wouldn't shut off for two seconds. I popped a Benadryl around nine. By midnight it still hadn't kicked in, so I brewed a cup of Sleepy Time Tea and chewed a melatonin tab out of desperation. I managed to get approximately four hours of sleep, but now I'm feeling worse than if I'd have downed a bottle of wine and passed out. I'd still feel hungover, but the process might have been a little more enjoyable.

I grab a cinnamon dolce pod from the Keurig carousel and pop it in. Sliding my phone from my pocket, I aimlessly tap on apps. Texts and emails are all caught up. Social media is same old random nothingness.

My coffee finishes, the machine squirting out the last few drops in good faith, and I return to the sofa beside my nieces. Outside, the wind blows hard against the house, whistling through the windows and creating near white-out conditions every time there's a gust, but the moments when it settles, it's the most beautiful thing with some of the biggest snowflakes I've ever seen.

Taking a sip, I wrap my palms around the mug and think about whether or not I want to turn the fireplace on. It's gas, and Cole can be such a cheap ass sometimes. Never mind that he's an industrial engineer who commutes to work in a Mercedes SUV, but that's none of my business ...

or at least that's what my sister tells me when I tease her about it.

The girls are holding hands, glued to Angelina Ballerina with giant smiles on their faces, and it's quite possibly one of the cutest things I've ever seen in my entire life, so I grab my phone and snap a picture, sending it to my parents, Neve and her husband, and my brother, Logan. When I'm finished, I add the picture to my E + E album on my phone … only instead of closing out of the app, my thumb hovers over another album: RY.

Reed York.

Why I haven't brought myself to delete them yet, I'm not sure, but there they are. All five hundred pictures from our numerous weekend romps and sex-cations. I suppose it's not the worst thing in the world that I kept them. There are no pictures of the two of us. Selfies were always against our self-made rules.

Thumbing through the album, my gaze lingers on pristine beaches, rolling vineyards, and cliché snaps of some of the most amazing dinners I've had the privilege of enjoying.

And while Reed might not be in any of the photos, his presence is undeniable. Invisibly imprinted, almost. It's just … there.

The screech and rattle of the garage doors signal that someone's home, and a minute later, my sister strolls in, dropping her bag and keys on the kitchen counter. The girls fling their shared blanket off their laps and run into her arms like they didn't just see her a couple of hours ago, and I pause the movie before joining them in the kitchen.

"How were they?" Neve asks, hoisting Ellison on one hip with practiced ease.

"Do you even have to ask that question at this point?" I wink, taking a sip of my coffee as I lean against the island.

"Mom wants to know if you're bringing that guy over for Christmas dinner."

My brows rise before narrowing. "That's random. And what guy?"

"The one you were dating."

"Jeremiah? The one I went on two dates with last month before he blew me off after Thanksgiving so he could go Black Friday shopping with his ex-girlfriend? *That* guy?" I scoff. "Please feel free to inform our mother that no, I will not be bringing *that guy* to our Christmas dinner."

Neve laughs. "You know Mom. Ever the hopeless romantic."

I take another drink, trying to remember the last time I knew what romance felt like. Had to have been three years ago, when I was still with my ex from college. He was always sending me flowers randomly. And on the nights I worked late, he'd always have dinner ready for me when I got home—usually takeout or pizza, but still. It was sweet, I guess. Though just once, I think I'd like to know what a grand, romantic gesture is like. Nothing cheesy, just something that means something expressed in a way that's never been done before.

I don't think it's too much to ask.

"What are you thinking about?" my sister asks, letting her daughter slide down her hip. Ellison runs back to the family room with her sister in tow. "You're doing that thing where you chew the inside of your lip and get this far-off look in your eyes."

I've never breathed a word of anything Reed-related to anyone in my family. When things were kosher, it wasn't like I felt the need to mention to my family that I had a "fuck buddy," and when things were bad and I moved home, I never felt the need to go into detail about the events surrounding my transfer.

No sense in rehashing the past now, even if the past is probably palling around my city this very moment.

Shaking my head, I say, "It's nothing. Honestly. Anyway, I need to stop at the mall and grab a Secret Santa gift. Office party is Monday night."

"Fun, fun." Neve smiles. "Behave yourself now. Don't get too turned up or whatever the saying is."

"Neve, stop. Your Middle-Aged Mom is starting to show."

"Hush." She swats her hand at me as I grab my coat off the back of a kitchen chair.

A minute later, I'm bundled for the cold and digging my keys out of my bag. "See you Thursday. Don't forget, I'm bringing the pie."

Neve walks me out, and I dash to my car through blowing snow gusts and wind so ice-cold it could snap my bones if I stay out here too long. It's times like these I miss LA. Those lucky bastards are still sipping cocktails on outdoor patios this time of year, listening to live music so vibrant even the palm trees can't help but sway to the beat.

I start my car a few seconds later and let the engine warm, lingering in the driveway until the heat kicks on. Cranking it full blast, I wait until the icy build-up on my windshield is melted before pulling out and heading straight for the Mills Haven Shopping Center.

This year I drew Jodi's name, and while she works in a different department and telecommutes half the time, I can't help but notice she's always wearing charm bracelets. A quick stop at one of those charm bracelet stores at the mall should suffice.

Snow collects on my window as I drive, and I hit the

wipers, smearing the melting mess until it's clear again. A Michael Bublé Christmas song plays softly on the radio, instantly making my skin hot and itchy. It reminds me of something, though I'm not sure what. I flick to a different station, settling on an old Bing Crosby holiday standard, and three songs later, I pull into the crowded mall parking lot.

It only takes twenty minutes to find a spot, and I almost get into a turn-signal war with a Rudolph nose and antler-wearing Dodge Caravan, but fortunately a second spot opens up, saving the day.

It's a Christmas miracle.

Once inside, the place is elbow-to-stroller-to-shopping bag packed, but I manage to make it to the charm bracelet store on the north side in good time. I choose a star-shaped charm with tiny Swarovski crystals. It's generic enough that I think she'll like it, but it's also sparkly and perfect for this time of year.

I tuck the little bag inside my purse and head back to the parking lot, dreaming about fuzzy socks and fleece pajamas and finishing The Family Stone as soon as I get home, but it hits me somewhere between Greenbriar Parkway and Beckwith Avenue that chances are Reed is going to be invited to our holiday party Monday evening.

Not only will I have to see him all day that day, but I'll be forced to extend my cordiality into the evening. That plus alcohol plus all the words I've been swallowing over the past could be a lethal combination.

Gripping the steering wheel, I crank the radio and finish my drive home with the tightest of knots in my center and the tiniest voice in my head insisting that there's no possible way this is going to go well—for either of us.

PAST

Joa

"Mexican or Italian?" I yell from the bed of our rented condo in Miami.

Reed is in the shower.

I haven't yet bothered to get dressed, just sitting here with the sheets wrapped around me while I look up local restaurants that deliver.

"Chinese," he yells back. "But check the reviews on Yelp before you pick one."

I roll my eyes. Sometimes he can be so ... extra.

The door to the bathroom is slightly open, filling the bedroom with muggy steam that smells like him. Cedar and vetiver. Musk and sex.

This is our second trip together. Last month we went to the Catalina Islands for three days and stayed at some renovated cottage in the back of someone's massive estate.

He was serious about the hotel thing, though he refuses to

elaborate. Every time I try to bring it up, he shuts it down with a smart-assed remark.

At this point, I've stopped caring. And honestly, he's so generously paying for the AirBnbs so at the end of the day, it's only fair that he chooses the place.

I have to admit, I was a bit nervous last month when we took our first trip together. I kept overanalyzing every little thing I said. The way I was sitting or if I touched him too much or gave off any impression that I was trying to veer us toward boyfriend/girlfriend territory.

After the first night, I realized that by acting all self-conscious, I was inadvertently acting like a nervous new girlfriend, and I promptly changed my entire modus operandi from that point on.

It's actually kind of nice, not having the confines and pressures of an actual relationship.

There are no important dates to memorize.

No gifts to give.

No parents to meet.

No arguing over movies since we don't see them together.

And I like the fact that we don't go to each other's places. When Reed first proposed that, at first I thought maybe he had a wife or girlfriend and was trying to hide me from what-ever it was he had going on at home, but I've recently become close with one of the other girls in the office, and she wasted no time giving me the full scoop on Mr. Reed York.

He's not married. He's a commitment-phobic LA bach-elor who loves his job more than he'll ever love a woman.

In other words, he's as single as they come and he couldn't be further from my type—which means this whole arrangement is actually pretty perfect for me.

All of that said, I couldn't help but see the tiniest bit of red the other day when I saw Heather from IT trying to chat him up at the copier.

I was on the other side of the office, watching from afar, so I'm not even sure what they were talking about. For all I know, they could've been discussing last night's episode of Game of Thrones. But his smile to her was like a punch in the gut to me—one that I absolutely was not expecting.

I forced it away.

I knew better than to feel any sort of ownership toward him.

Reed emerges from the shower, and I'm already on the phone, ordering his favorite General Tsao's chicken with brown rice and crab rangoon. We've had enough takeout dinners that I know all of his preferences across varying cuisines.

It's funny.

I could tell you that he loves rigatoni primavera from Paolo's. I could tell you that he loves the butter chicken from India Star but not the butter chicken from Namaste. I could tell you he loves the chicken fajitas in corn tortillas with no onions and a side of salsa verde from Guadalajara's.

But I couldn't tell you his parents' name.

Or if he has any siblings.

Or where he went to college.

Curiosity gnaws away at me sometimes, when I'm lying in bed next to him, jetlagged and unable to sleep.

It's only natural to want to know things about people, to want to find out who they are underneath their carefully crafted exterior.

But if I ask too many questions, he'll get the wrong idea. He'll think I'm asking to meet his parents or that I'm trying to get closer to him by getting to know him better.

So I'll keep my questions to myself.

We've got a good little thing going here.
I don't want to jeopardize it.

6

REED

THERE'S something cliché about a suited executive carrying two dozen glazed Krispy Kremes into an office on a Monday morning, but it is what it is. I've never met ten out of eleven of the employees here, and I'm sure they're all on edge. I figured I'd start the day with a quick meeting and a sugar high and go from there.

"Reed?" A man with thinning hair and smiling eyes appears from an office doorway.

"Yes."

"Harold Coffey. Nice to finally meet you in person." He extends his right hand, and I move the boxes to my left arm, meeting his handshake with the kind of firmness that lets him know I'm in charge here ... just in case he's one of those asses with the big heads who think they run the show just because they've got the words "branch manager" in their title.

"Good to meet you as well. Point me to the conference room?" I ask.

It's early, about a half hour before most of the staff gets here, but I wanted to get a head start on setting up for the meeting.

And I wanted to be here before Joa got in.

"Right this way." Harold takes the donuts and leads me down a hall, flicking on lights in the process. When we get to the end, he retrieves a set of keys from his pocket and impressively jams one into the lock with a single hand. "Here we are."

The room is small. A ten-foot table with maybe twelve chairs centers the space, and a wall of windows provides a gray cityscape view clouded with fog and an even grayer sky.

I can't believe she traded palm trees for this shit.

Sliding my leather messenger bag down my arm, I place it on the table and take a seat at the head.

"I'll just work from here, if you don't mind," I tell Harold.

"Of course. We've got a spare office if you'd like that too, but wherever you're comfortable is fine." He smiles. In fact, I don't think he's stopped smiling since I got here. It's not natural to smile that much. I don't care who you are, no one is that happy all of the time.

I'm going to give him the benefit of the doubt and chalk it up to nerves.

Everyone gets nervous when one of the big dogs comes to town. The New York branch is the worst. They walk around all stiff-shouldered and shifty-eyed, their demeanors instantly on the defense like *I'm* the jerk who dared show up at one of the branches whose finances I oversee.

"I'll let you do your thing," Harold says, his fingertips

tapping together as he lingers in the doorway of the conference room. "Everyone should be in around eight. I'll send them down here shortly after that and we can get started."

He messes with his tie for a second before flashing another smile and leaving.

Nerves.

Definitely nerves.

And he should be nervous.

I'm not here for a friendly hello. I'm here because shit's about to hit the fan. But until I get the green light, I'm not at liberty to discuss that with anyone here. And in the meantime, I'll get this quick meet-and-greet over with, do my thing, and go from there.

"Hi."

I glance up and find an older woman with salt-and-pepper hair and a magenta sweater standing in the doorway.

"I'm Pam. You must be Mr. York?" she asks as she shuffles in, a yellow pad and gel pen in one hand and a mug of coffee in the other.

I check my watch.

"I always get here early," she says with a chuckle. "I like to put a pot of coffee on so it's fresh when everyone else gets in."

She's got the Midwestern, nice-for-no-reason thing going on, and I can appreciate that—as long as she doesn't dawdle and waste my time with unnecessary small talk.

"Very thoughtful of you," I say, turning my attention to my email.

"Would you like me to make you a cup?" she asks.

Oh, Pam.

I want to like you.

Please let me like you ...

I glance up and make myself offer a tight smile. Small talk has never been my thing, but I know she's simply trying to be hospitable. "No thank you."

She settles into her chair, flipping her notebook to a clean page when two more ladies walk in, followed by a fresh-faced kid in a too-big suit. Two more suits walk in. Harold returns. Another woman. I count them all. Seven. We're missing three more plus Joa.

My throat constricts just enough for me to notice. I swear it's grown a little warmer in here in the last few minutes.

Two more women enter the room, napkins and paper plates in hand. One of them carries a carton of orange juice and a stack of cups. Do they just have that stuff lying around?

Another man walks in, dressed in gray slacks and a purple sweater.

That leaves Joa.

Of course she's taking her sweet time. She's probably doing it on purpose just to torture me, that little minx.

I smirk to myself, chin tucked, then I glance up.

And just like that ... she's ten feet in front of me, lingering in the doorway of the now-filled conference room. A notebook is clutched against her chest, a pen in her fist. Her baby blues scan the room in search of an empty seat, and when she realizes the only one left is the one to my right, she releases a little sigh no one seems to notice but me.

I rise, extending my hand toward the chair. "Joa, good to see you again. It's been a while."

All eyes are on the two of us.

Her stone-cold stare holds mine and in that short span of a few endless seconds, it feels like there's so much that needs to be said, but she clears her throat, slides her hands under her skirt, and takes a seat next to me.

The sweet scent of her perfume fills the air around us and my cock throbs, like a fucking Pavlovian dog that's been classically conditioned.

Taking my seat again, I rest my elbows on the table, the cuff of my suit coat pulling back just enough to expose the charcoal leather band and shiny platinum face of my Burberry watch.

From the corner of my eye, I feel the drift of her gaze and watch the way her thumb presses against the ballpoint pen in her right hand.

I knew she'd notice. She always did have a penchant for detail.

Pretending I'm oblivious, I smooth my hand along my tie—the one from our *first* time. The one I used to tie her wrists more times than I can count.

"Now that Ms. Jolivet has made her arrival, we can begin." I don't look at her this time, but I can almost feel her shooting daggers my way. "Forgive me for being all kinds of cliché today, but if you could just go around the table and introduce yourselves, that'd be great. And please help yourself to a donut if you haven't yet."

Joa leans back in her chair, long legs crossed, and a scrutinizing glare pointed at me.

I deserve that.

"Why don't we start with you?" I ask the blonde with the thick glasses seated across from Joa.

"Lucy Clarke, Accounts Receivable," she says before the next one takes her turn.

Jodi.

Piper.

Harold.

Richard.

Sam.

Carol-Ann.

Kennedy.

Pam.

Linc.

And back to Joa.

"All right. Thanks everyone," I say. "I know you're all wondering what I'm doing here and why I came on such short notice."

The room is so quiet I can hear the woman beside me swallow the lump in her throat before reaching for a glass of orange juice.

"I've been tasked with performing an end-of-year audit on a few of our accounts, and in doing so, I'm going to be pulling a few of you aside for some questions." I try to keep it as brief and to the point as I can. Panic isn't going to help anything, nor will it change the outcome of the investigation. "I'd very much appreciate it if you would all carry on as per usual in the meantime."

Harold wipes his pudgy fingers on a napkin before messing with his tie. He's the only one who can't seem to sit still out of this entire group. I can't be certain, but from this end of the table it almost looks like he's beginning to sweat, then again, it is rather warm and we're in a bit of a confined space.

"I'll be working from the conference room this week," I say, "if anyone needs me. Otherwise, you're all free to go."

"That's it?" Someone—Kennedy maybe—blurts out from down the line.

"Excuse me?" I ask.

"You came out here last minute during the week of Christmas just to audit some accounts?" The woman gathers her things, shaking her head. "I'm sorry, Mr. York. You seriously can't expect us to carry on *as per usual* when something is clearly going on behind the scenes. If our jobs are on the line, you owe it to us to tell us right now."

My jaw tightens. She has a point, but I'm not in a position to speak on this just yet or to veer too far from my script. Foolishly, I'd hoped that these people would be so caught up in their pre-holiday busy-ness that they'd hope for the best and leave the questions to a minimum.

"Are we closing down?" someone else asks.

"We had record numbers last quarter. There's no way," one of the suits adds.

"Is this because we lost the Hyperion account?" another woman asks.

I place my palm up. "Everyone, if you could please return to your offices and get to work, I can begin my audit. The sooner I'm finished, the sooner we'll know—"

"—the sooner we'll know if we're all being canned," someone else finishes my sentence.

Scanning the room, I run a quick head count. We're down to nine. A quick glance to my left and I realize Joa's missing. She must have snuck out the moment I dismissed everyone. But who's the other one?

Harold.

Interesting.

"Everyone, if you don't mind, I'd like to get started." I walk to the door, hoping the herd will follow. It takes a few seconds, and I get a handful of curious looks, but eventually they shuffle out into the hall and scatter to their offices.

Returning to the table, I lift the lid of my laptop and take care of a handful of emails, a Monday morning report for the senior leadership team, and hop on a Zoom call with

New York. By the time I'm finished, it's nearly noon—the past three hours gone, just like that.

Getting up, I stretch my legs and go for a walk around the office. I've never seen such a diligent and hardworking crew. No one's socializing. No one's hanging out by the coffee maker. Everyone's got their eyes glued to their computer screens and their fingers pecking away at their keyboards.

They must take me for a moron if they think I'm going to believe this is how it always is, but honestly, I couldn't care less. It's not why I'm here and I'm certainly not an executive babysitter, so they can stop with the act. It isn't fooling anyone.

"Excuse me," I say when I get to the lady with the purple sweater. She's seated at the front desk, sorting mail and paperclipping bundles together. "Pam? Is it?"

"Yes! How can I help you?"

"Could you direct me to Ms. Jolivet's office, please?"

Her gray eyes graze my shoulder and she points. "Right behind you."

The door is closed and the lights are off.

"But you just missed her," Pam says.

"Do you know when you expect her back?"

Her mouth twists at the side. "It's hard to say. It's a client lunch, so it could be an hour or it could be a little longer. I'd be happy to come and get you the second she walks in."

Exhaling, I knock on her desktop with my knuckles. "That'd be great. Thank you."

All I wanted to do was offer an appropriate hello, feel her out, and ensure her that the rest of the week needn't be tense and awkward. It might be a long shot but if I could just get her to talk to me, maybe ... just maybe she'll loosen her grip on that grudge she's been holding onto for the past year and we can make an inkling of progress.

But I guess it'll have to wait.

Heading back to the conference room, I peer out the window to the sidewalk three stories below, where a black Escalade is parked just outside the main entrance.

A moment later, a woman in a pencil skirt and wool coat brushes her long black hair over her shoulder and waves at someone in the car. A uniformed driver appears from the other side of the SUV, getting the rear door so a silver-fox-type in a gray trench coat over black slacks appears, wearing a smile so wide I'm sure you could see it from the International Space Station.

The woman turns for a second, pointing to the building, her lips moving.

It's Joa.

The man laughs at whatever it was she said before narrowing the divide between them and leaning in to kiss her cheek.

Seriously, Joa?

Normally in our line of work, we're the ones doing the wooing—not the other way around.

I watch the two of them climb in the backseat together, my blood beginning to simmer, and then I watch them drive away.

All this time, I'd expected her to move on.

I just didn't think I'd ever have to see it firsthand.

"Mr. York?" Pam knocks on the conference room door.

"Yes, Pam?"

"I was going to tell you ... our office holiday party is tonight after work. It's pretty informal. We're just grabbing drinks at a bar down the street and exchanging gifts—

though you wouldn't need to bring anything for that—would you like to join us?" she asks.

Suffering through an office party with a bunch of strangers sounds like my idea of fresh hell, but it might be my only opportunity to corner Joa, especially if she's had a couple of drinks and lets her guard down.

"I'd love to, Pam," I say. "Count me in."

PAST

Reed

"Make it quick," she whispers as we stumble into the ladies' room at some French place in downtown LA after work.

The whole team is here. Grosvenor insisted on taking us all out for a celebratory dinner since GenCoin surpassed ten grand this week.

It's been five days since our last hookup.

Five days too long.

Ordinarily I'm a patient man, but I couldn't tonight, not with this off-the-shoulder number she's wearing and that sun-kissed collarbone and the way she kept eye fucking me from the end of the table.

But it wasn't until some asshole in a three-piece suit sent her a drink from the bar that I almost lost my cool.

Despite the fact that she's very much not my girlfriend, the thought of anyone else so much as thinking about touching her makes me rage a little on the inside.

I managed to rein it back enough because I'm nothing if

not in control of myself, and as soon as I composed myself, I sent her a quick text telling her to meet me by the bathrooms.

"Did you lock the door?" she asks.

"I'm horny, not a moron."

"They're going to notice we're gone," she says as I lift her onto the table.

"So?" I shove her dress up her thighs and slip her panties off. "Let them."

I press my mouth against hers and her fingers lace through my hair as she kisses me back.

We finish in under five minutes—obviously a record for myself—and when we've made ourselves presentable, we dash out of the restroom with matching flushes on our faces, returning to the table just as they're serving the main course.

One of the women from another department, whose name is irrelevant to me, stares with judgy eyes at Joa then to me and back. I give her a wink and she quickly looks away, clearing her throat and reaching for her water.

The details of our arrangement are none of her business, and neither are the things we do when we're alone together.

From my end of the table, I feel a fresh set of eyes directed toward me, and I glance up just long enough to catch Joa staring, looking lost in thought almost.

A second later, she reaches for her martini glass and turns to the woman sitting next to her, attempting to pretend I didn't just catch her in the act.

While part of me would love to know what she was thinking just then, most of me knows I'm better off letting it go.

We've got a good thing going.

And I intend to keep it that way for as long as humanly possible—or at least until I get sick of her or she decides she wants a relationship and shows herself the door like they always do.

What can I say? I'm a man of my word.

Besides, I suck at the whole love bullshit, and Joa deserves someone who can love her right—at least when the time comes.

For now? She's mine.

7

Joa

"WHAT ARE YOU THINKING, red or white today?" My client, David Crosswhite, CEO of Crosswhite Holdings, peruses the wine menu.

Day drinking isn't my thing and the office party is tonight, but customarily I'm supposed to go along with him.

Anything for the client has always been the Genesis way.

"I love a dry white, but I'll have what you're having," I say with a smile.

"Sauvignon blanc. My kind of girl." He winks, folding the menu and handing it to our server. "Dry white it is. Why don't you bring us a bottle of the Cascade Falls, 1999 if you have it."

"Excellent choice." The waiter leaves.

"You didn't have to order an entire bottle," I say, unfolding my napkin and laying it across my skirt.

The restaurant fills with noon hour reservationists, and

a string quartet plays *Deck the Halls* from the next room. The clink of silver on china fills the pauses between us.

"Don't be ridiculous. You've been so good to me this year, Joa. It's my treat." He reaches across the table, almost as if he intends to place his hand over mine, and then he stops. His fingers curl slightly and he glances away.

He's been trying to date me since six months ago, after our first meeting. And while he's handsome and worldly and charming in his own way, he's also nearly twice my age, thrice divorced, and a father of five, ages three to twenty-five. Fortunately for me, he's the opposite of aggressive—which undermines every assumption I've ever made about him.

"Joa, I can't tell you how pleased I am with my portfolio's performance this year," he says when the waiter returns with a green bottle, a corkscrew, and a promise to be right back once he pours our glasses. "It's been one of our best yet. And we owe it all to you."

"Thank you," I say. "I've worked especially hard on yours, tweaking and perfecting those ratios. It's all about timing, luck, and some good old-fashioned optimization."

The Crosswhite account is the biggest of my bunch by leaps and bounds—the one I'd lose my job over should anything remotely go wrong. I protect it like a bar swallow guards her nest.

"Does Genesis give you much time off over the holidays?" he asks, lifting his glass to mine.

We clink our chalices and take sips.

"Just Christmas Day and New Year's Day," I say, scanning the restaurant. I'm not sure why, but I keep half-expecting Reed to show up.

He wouldn't—desperation has never been his style. But I can't help but look for him anyway.

This morning was … interesting, to say the least. He stood in front of the entire staff claiming he's simply here for an audit, yet he was wearing the watch I picked out for him and the tie we used many a time as a makeshift restraint.

And his signature Creed cologne.

Oh, god. Why did he have to wear *the* cologne?

Heat creeps up my neck and I pray that if I'm blushing, David doesn't notice. It's dark enough in here that he shouldn't—the only real light around us stems from flickering tea light candles placed in crystal holders next to clipped red rose centerpieces.

I didn't realize how romantic this place is.

"Are we ready to order?" Our server returns.

I hadn't even glanced at the menu.

David looks to me, his dark gray brows lifted. "Joa, I'd be happy to order for the two of us if that's okay with you?"

Anything for the client …

"Sure. Thank you." I fold my hands in my lap, hoping he doesn't go crazy.

"We'll start with the tuna tartare small plates," he says. "After that, we'll do the arugula house salad and lobster bisque. Two filets for the entrée. And for dessert?" He scratches his chin, his lips pressed into a thin line. "Vanilla bean crème brûlée."

"Wonderful. I'll put these in, and your small plates should be out shortly." The server leaves, and I sit in stunned silence as I realize we're going to be here all afternoon.

On one hand, I'm okay with that. More time here means less time back at the office. But on the other hand, I'm going to have to be rolled out of here Violet-Beauregard style on top of spending the next several hours nonchalantly ignoring David's advances.

"That's quite a feast you ordered us," I say, fingers resting on the stem of my glass. As long as I go slow and pace myself, I should still be able to walk into the party tonight with all my merits intact.

"A celebration calls for a feast, don't you think?" he asks.

When he emailed me last week asking if I was available Monday at noon, he mentioned a "little celebratory lunch." To me that means a quick forty-five minutes at a popular hustling and bustling lunchtime spot up the street—not a five-course meal at one of the most exclusive restaurants in the city.

"How are the little ones?" I ask.

"D.J. is about to turn four next month," he says with a smile. "It's all he'll talk about anymore. That and Thomas the Train. Vivica's excited for Christmas morning. Think we've got one more year of her believing in Santa."

He doesn't mention the older three. Never does. They're from his first marriage, and from what I can gather, they still haven't forgiven him for leaving their mother. It's strange for me to think of classy, well-mannered David embroiled in personal drama, but I suppose no one's immune to it.

"Their mother is letting me sleep in the guesthouse Christmas Eve. I'll be there to watch the whole thing," he says with a proud beam. "You have any plans?"

This conversation is killing me. A slow, innocent death.

He's a kind man with a huge heart and decent intentions aside from his own personal demons, but there's no chemistry between us. In fact, there's less than no chemistry between us. There's negative chemistry.

He might as well be my uncle because when I look at him, that's the way I feel. He's an older man whom I respect. That's it.

"Going to my parents' house in Mills Haven," I say.

"Ah, Mills Haven. That's a nice little community. I've done business there. Is that where you grew up?"

I nod, stifling a yawn.

Once again, I slept maybe a grand total of four or five hours last night, marking three nights in a row of little to no sleep. The alcohol mixed with the cozy ambience around us and the gentle stringed music playing in the background is all but taunting me with the fact that I couldn't go home and take a nap even if I wanted to.

A food runner deposits a small plate of tuna tartare and David's face is awash in delight, boyish excitement almost. I guess it's the little things for him.

Fending off another yawn, I remind myself that I could be in worse company.

PAST

Joa

"Why didn't you tell me you were staying late tonight?" Reed stands in my office doorway on a Tuesday night, his jacket slung over his shoulder. "Want some company? I'm meeting some friends in an hour, but I can spare a little time."

Before I have a chance to explain that I'm doing actual work tonight, work that requires my undivided, non-distracted attention, he's closing my door, strutting across the room, and sliding his hands over my shoulders, kneading the knots until the pain and tension dissipates.

God, why does he have to be so good with his hands?

Gently, I push his hands from my shoulders. "Tonight's no good."

He laughs. "What do you mean tonight's no good?"

We've been hooking up four months now and not once have I ever rebuffed him, not once have I ever not wanted him.

But this is serious.

I'm trying to land one of my biggest clients ever, and this portfolio presentation has to be better than perfect.

"I'm busy." *I point to my monitor.*

"Yes, Joa, I see that you're working on a spreadsheet right now, but I don't see how that's different from any other time we ..."

I spin in my desk chair, facing him. "It's nothing personal."

"Of course it is."

I've never seen him like this before. Normally he lets things roll off his back, dusts his shoulders off, and carries on like nothing happened.

"For real. I need to get this done and I don't want to be here all night. I'll see you tomorrow, okay? Have fun with your friends."

He doesn't budge, doesn't blink. He just stands there taking me in with this slightly squinted look on his face.

I need this client.

I need to prove to Grosvenor that I'm learning and growing and willing to work twice as hard as anyone else around here because I just got word that our VP of Acquisitions is retiring and I want her job like I've never wanted anything else in my twenty-seven years.

Landing this client would be huge, not only for me but for Genesis as a whole.

Grosvenor would practically be obligated to promote me, especially if he doesn't want to lose me.

"Have fun with my friends?" *Reed echoes my sentiment.*

Maybe I said it a little too harshly. Maybe it came off sarcastic or curt, I don't know. However I said it clearly bothers him or he wouldn't be standing here trying to read between two lines that only exist in his current state of insecurity.

I decide to cut him some slack.

Everyone has off days.

Lord knows I've had my fair share.

"I meant it in a nice way. I wasn't trying to be flippant," I assure him. "And what's with you overanalyzing this conversation? Shouldn't you be halfway to your car by now? Thinking about the part of your life that doesn't revolve around screwing your colleague every chance you get?"

"You've just been different lately."

"And what makes you think it has anything to do with you?" I say with an incredulous, breathy laugh as I cross my arms and cross my legs and lean back in my chair. "I've been pouring my heart and soul into this project and I'm meeting with the client tomorrow afternoon, so if you don't mind, I'd really love to finish this so I can go home and get at least six hours of sleep."

My voice is louder than I meant for it to be, my body clenched so hard my abdomen burns.

I've never yelled at him, never snapped.

In fact, we've never fought.

Bickered, yes.

Bantered, always.

But never an actual fight.

"I'll see you in the morning. Good luck with everything." Reed shows himself out before I have a chance to apologize, and despite the fact that I need every minute I can squeeze out of this evening, there's a piece of me that wishes he'd come back, put me in my place, kiss me hard against the back of the door.

I don't know what that was about, but he's gone now, and I don't have time to give it another thought.

I let it go.

I'm ninety-nine percent sure he'll walk in here tomorrow like nothing happened and everything will be back to normal.

And if he doesn't? I'll apologize for yelling, but I won't apologize for putting my work before ... extracurriculars.

Before him.

My job is my future.

Reed York isn't.

8

REED

"PAM SAID you were looking for me?" Joa stands at the threshold of the conference room, favoring the hall side, her hands braced against the door jamb. Everything about her says she's trying like hell to physically resist me.

I take my time checking my watch. "Do you always take three-hour lunches?"

Her arms tighten across her chest. "I was with a client."

"Do you always let your clients kiss you?"

Her jaw hangs loose. "You were watching me?"

"Not watching. I looked outside and happened to see. Joa, why don't you come in and shut the door."

She hesitates, nostrils slightly flared, and then her arms drop to her sides and she exhales before stepping inside and shutting the door.

"You don't have to stand all the way over there." I chuff, finding amusement in the fact that she's still digging her heels in. "I'm not going to bite. Only did that once. You didn't like it, remember?"

"I can't believe we're having this conversation right now."

"I can't believe we're having a conversation, period." I rise, buttoning my suit coat as I make my way to her. "And I also can't believe I had to fly two thousand miles across the country to get you to even look at me."

"Really? Reed? You *can't believe* that?" Her tone is mocking, her angled brows a stark contrast on her sweet face. She's never been good at looking angry. It doesn't suit her.

"All I wanted to do that day was tell you how sorry I was—"

"—sorry?!" She laughs, refusing to let me explain that my hands were tied. I was tapped that morning and told I had no choice but to take a job for which I never applied—a job that I didn't even want—and that was before I knew the half of what was going on. "You were sorry? You wished me luck that morning, Reed. And then you took the job right out from under me. You knew how much I wanted that job and you just ... took it. And then you stand here a year later with the audacity to act like I owe you a chance to apologize."

"You don't owe me anything, Joa."

Her lips part, as if she already had a response prepared, but she stops herself, apparently at a loss for words. And I could be imagining this, but I swear her expression softened just a hair.

"Look—" I begin to say until she waves her hand through the air to silence me.

"Please. Let's not waste our time talking about something that happened a lifetime ago," she says. Funny how a year ago feels like a lifetime to her. It feels like only yesterday to me. "And by the way, you told Coffey you wanted me to be your 'right hand gal' while you're in town. Unfortunately, you're going to have to find someone else. If you think for one second I'm going to *help* you do *anything*, you're delusional."

"Fair enough." It was nothing more than a test anyway. I don't need her help. I simply needed to see how she'd react at the idea of having to work with me again.

I got my answer.

"So what was it you needed from me?" she asks, her words rushed and laced in impatience. "Why did you tell Pam to send me in here? If it's not work-related, I'd really like to get back to my desk and finish up some emails before I leave for the day."

She won't look at me now, she'll only stare through me, doing that thing where she chews on the inside of her lip while looking lost in thought.

What I wouldn't give to know what she's thinking about.

"I just had a few questions for my audit," I say. "But seeing how you've been gone most of the afternoon, I'll let you get back to work. We'll reconvene in the morning."

Without saying a word, she turns and leaves, closing the door behind her, which almost feels like a metaphor.

I watch through the glass walls of the conference room until she disappears down the hall.

Unbuttoning my jacket, I take a seat, finish up a few emails, and pack up for the day. Stopping by the front desk, I ask Pam for the address of the bar they're meeting at, and then I head back to the AirBnB to get ready for tonight.

God, it felt good to hear her voice again.

Now if I could just taste that cinnamon pout, it'll be a Christmas miracle.

PAST

Reed

"Do you believe in aliens?" Joa rests her cheek against my bare chest as we lay in bed at some rental house in Sedona.

"That's random."

"I've always associated Arizona with weird stuff. UFOs and Area 51. My dad is secretly obsessed with that kind of stuff. Guess it rubbed off on me a bit."

"I don't believe in things I can't experience with at least one of my five senses."

She traces the tip of her fingernail down the center of my abs, following the ridges and indentations.

"My sister once claimed she saw a ghost. We were staying over at my grandparents' house. This old farmhouse built in the eighteen hundreds. And she saw this lady in a white dress walk out of the forest beside the house and then she just ... disappeared."

"I'm sure she was imagining it."

"If you knew Neve, you'd know she's not the type to

make this kind of thing up. In fact, it took her three years to tell anyone about it because she was so sure no one would believe her."

I sit up, gently moving her off of my naked body. "I'm going to hit the shower."

"You really don't believe in anything?" she asks as I slide out from the covers.

"Guess not."

"That's kind of sad, Reed."

Turning, I say, "Please, save your tears for some other asshole."

"Hasn't anything wonderful ever happened to you? Unexplained or otherwise?" She gathers the covers around her. "Sometimes I think about the size of the universe and I get overwhelmed." Glancing down, she shrugs her shoulders. "I've never told anyone that before."

"Lucky me."

Her pale blues lift onto mine. "Ass."

"If you're done picking my brain with your random, woo-woo philosophical questions, then I'd like to take a shower."

She waves me on and I head into the en-suite, shutting the door behind me. A minute later, when I'm standing under a spray of hot water, I contemplate her question and the reason I never gave her a straight answer.

Even with all the luxuries and advantages I've been afforded in my thirty years, my life has been remarkably unwonderful.

I've never told anyone that before, and I don't intend to start now.

9

Joa

FRIAR PARSON'S on 8th street is a madhouse at happy hour, but they've reserved their private party room for the eleven of us tonight.

"How are we doing tonight?" Our personal cocktail waitress, who happens to be dressed like a nun, greets our group.

Pam raises a hand in the air like she's waiting to be called on. "Um, yes, Sister. Ma'am. Can we get one more chair please? We've added another guest."

"Of course." The nun leaves our private room and I lean into Lucy.

"Please, please, please tell me Reed's not ..." I don't get to finish my sentence.

The man of the hour has arrived.

His ocean eyes scan the small room, stopping when they find me. The seats on either side of me are occupied, but the spot across from me is vacant because Richard got up to use the restroom and didn't think to leave any kind of indication that the spot was taken.

"So glad you could make it," Pam tells him.

God, she's really been up his ass today, but that's her. Always so ... *extra*.

"Thanks for the invite," he says to her, though he's looking at me.

The nun returns with an extra chair, sticking it between Kennedy and Piper.

"All right. Let's get these orders going," she says. "What are we drinking?"

She starts with Piper and by the time she gets to Harold, another nun arrives with a tray of communion-shaped shot glasses filled to the brim with what appears to be some kind of white liqueur garnished with chocolate sauce.

"Twelve candy canes," the second nun says, placing the tray in the center of the table.

"I don't think we ordered that, did we?" Pam asks.

"No. I did." Everyone looks to Reed. "First drinks are on me. I wanted to thank you all for such a warm welcome today." He looks to me. "And for including me tonight."

Yeah. *Thanks, Pam.*

Shots are passed down, everyone shooting theirs back the instant they get them, and I follow suit. The zip of peppermint Schnapps and the sweetness of the chocolate mix with the burn of the alcohol, but it goes down easily enough.

I came back to the office earlier today with a pretty intense buzz, and I crossed my fingers that Reed wouldn't notice.

And he didn't.

I think he was too focused on ... other things. At least that's all I can surmise by the fact that every time he thought I wasn't looking, his gaze would find all the parts of me he used to worship like a deity.

My thighs clench until they quiver.

I don't want to think about his tongue ... his hands ... his generous *endowment*.

"And how about you, my dear?" The nun makes her way to me. "What will we be having tonight?"

"I'll have a French 75, please. Thank you," I say, feeling the heaviness of Reed's attention.

"Some things never change," he says, tapping the cardboard coaster against the table as he wears a smirk.

"Exactly. Some things never change."

"Shall we exchange gifts now or later?" Harold asks. A couple of people shout "now" and the shuffling of gift wrap and tissue paper and paper bags fills the room.

I hand Jodi her wrapped charm.

Kennedy hands me a black-and-white striped bag with hot pink tissue paper. Digging in, I retrieve a three-wick Cucumber Melon candle from Bath and Body Works.

"Thanks, Ken!" I say, uncapping the jar and pretending to give it a good whiff. "I love it."

She gives me a thumbs' up from the other end of the table.

Reed wrinkles his nose. "You hate cucumber."

My eyes snap to his. He better hope Kennedy didn't hear him.

"Didn't anyone ever tell you it's the thought that counts?" I ask.

"Anyone ever tell you lying is rude?"

"Oh, you're one to talk." I cover my face with my hands for a second, gathering myself before I go off the deep end. The candy cane shot runs warm through my veins, and I feel my filter dissipating by the second.

Finally.

Drinks.

Three tray-carrying nuns pass out drinks, and it's only then that I notice Reed ordered a Manhattan. He always used to drink those when we'd travel, and I always used to make fun of him for being so stodgy and old-fashioned. When we were back in LA he'd order whiskey, Scotch, or the occasional beer, but his Manhattans were always reserved for getaways.

I never did ask him why.

Makes me think there's a lot I don't know about him.

But it's a moot point. And it's too late to care.

Reed takes a sip of his drink, peering over the top of his glass.

"You doing okay?" Lucy nudges me with her elbow.

Turning to her, I flash a smile. "I'm doing great."

Never better.

Her eyes narrow from behind her thick frames. She doesn't buy it for two seconds, but she knows better than to say a damn thing in front of our *guest*.

"Going to hit up the little nun's room," she says. "Want to come?"

I offer a polite 'no' and scoot my chair over so she can squeeze out. It's only then that I realize I've already downed over half of my cocktail and I don't even remember doing it. Shoving the glass away, I make a silent promise to pace myself.

Heat creeps up my neck, blooming in my cheeks and setting my skin on fire. I have no idea what's happening to me. All I know is I'm really freaking hot right now and I need some air. Springing up from the table, I leave my coat on the back of my chair, grab my phone, and head outside, bumping into Lucy on my way.

"Hey, you sure you're all right?" she asks, stopping me.

"Yep. Just wanted some fresh air. I'll be two seconds." I wedge my way through the crowded bar until I get to the main entrance. Dashing toward the snow-covered sidewalk, I welcome the ice-cold breaths and the freeze in my lungs that follows the second I step foot outside.

No clue what that was about and I'm sure I look like a crazy person standing out here in a skirt and heels and no jacket, but already I feel a million times better.

Wrapping my arms around my sides, I drag in a few more breaths, watching the clouds that fill the night air with each exhale.

"Joa."

Following a man's voice, I spin on my heels to find Reed standing outside the pub door, my jacket in his hands.

Oh, now he wants to be chivalrous? *Now?*

"Thought you might need this." He hands me my coat, which I promptly drape over my arm.

"You didn't have to do that."

The side of his mouth lifts into that perfect little half-smile that used to get me every time, and I force myself to look away.

"I know," he says.

"Okay … thanks …" I turn my back to him. I need five more minutes out here and then I'll head back in. Standing in silence, I listen for the shuffle of his shoes on concrete to indicate he's gone back inside, but I hear nothing. Dragging in another icicle of a breath, I turn to say something, only he's somehow … gone.

A quick chill nips at my nose, followed by a shiver that runs through my entire body. I expected a little more fight from him. A few more smart remarks. I was prepared for an emotional battle, armed with an arsenal of words.

The strangest niggle rests in my stomach, but I don't give it much more thought on the off chance it's something insane like ... *disappointment.*

I have no business being disappointed that he didn't stay out here. I should be pleased. Jumping up and down. Relieved if anything.

With my jacket in tow, I head back in, returning to my spot next to Lucy, across from an empty chair which held Reed only moments ago.

"Where'd he go?" I ask, letting my curiosity get the best of me.

Lucy shrugs. "I thought he was outside with you. I saw him grab your coat."

"Yeah, but he came back in."

"Why do you care?" She laughs, reaching for her martini.

"I don't. I'm just asking."

Lucy brings the glass to her ruby red lips. "Right."

A group of patrons stand outside our private room, beers in their hands as they discuss the Bears, but when I inspect the space beyond them, I see no sign of Reed. The man stands out like a sore thumb here with his sun-kissed complexion and his thick head of shiny, sandy blond hair. He's practically a human Ken doll complete with a Malibu pedigree.

I toss back what remains of my drink and head to the bar for a glass of ice water, and on the way, I inadvertently make eye contact with no less than six men.

I hate that I'm searching for Reed.

And I hate that I don't know why I'm searching for Reed.

But more than any of that, I hate the way my heart

hammers in my chest and my breath quickens the second I spot him at the bar.

Squeezing between a couple of customers a spot down from him, I flag down the bartender, grab my water, and try to get back to my table without being seen because odds are he's going to think I was looking for him, and we can't have that.

He'd get way too much satisfaction out of a notion as preposterous as that.

"Joa." A hand grips my arm, just above my elbow.

"Reed." I turn toward him.

"Where are you going?"

" ... back to the party ..."

"Stay. Have a drink with me. For old times' sake." He points toward his abandoned bar stool.

I'm not sure what he's smoking that makes him think I'd want to "have a drink for old times' sake," but I struggle to find the perfect response. It's like my words get lost on the way up any time he's around.

He releases his hold on my arm.

I release the breath I didn't know I was holding.

Without permission, my attention falls on his lips.

God, he was a good kisser. The best actually. We could make out for hours at a time, our jaws always tight and sore the next morning.

For the tiniest fraction of a second, I wonder how badly I'd hate myself if I were to let him kiss me tonight ...

But I won't. It goes against everything I've stood for over the past year. And what kind of message would that be sending if I let him waltz back in here and hand myself to him on a silver platter?

"I'm sorry, Reed," I say before heading back. "I think it's best that we not drink to old times."

PAST

Joa

I grip the handset of my desk phone with an unsteady fist, swiveling my chair so I face the cityscape view outside my office window as I call HR.

Palm trees.

Teslas, Ferraris, and Maseratis.

The joyful sun kissing a baby blue sky.

Outside it's an ordinary Los Angeles day in December, but inside, my traitorous colleague-with-benefits knocks on my locked office door.

"Open the door." The audacity of the desperation in his voice is only making it that much easier for me to hate him. "Please."

My fist tightens around the handset. How dare he pretend to care.

"Hi, Joa, how can I help you today?" Sheila answers.

"Is that division coordinator position still available? The one in Chicago?" I ask, unable to hide the breathlessness in

my voice. My chest caves with each lungful of peppermint-and-poinsettia-tinged office air, and my stomach twists in the tightest of knots.

The way I look at it, I have two options: I can stay here like a doormat, working beneath the man who knows every freckle of my body like the back of his hand—or I can go home to Illinois with my dignity intact, spend more time with my family, watch my nieces grow up in person and not via FaceTime, and attempt to convince myself the past eleven months were nothing more than a bad decision never to be repeated again.

"Yes, Joa, it is. Are you inter—" she begins to ask.

"—I'll take it. I can do an internal transfer, right?"

She pauses. Reed knocks on the door again and I glance toward the door without thinking. The outline of his broad shoulders and perfect head of hair makes a shadow against the interior blinds, a sight that mere hours ago would've sent a flutter to my middle and a half-bitten smile to my lips. I've run my fingers through that thick, sandy-blond mane more times than I can count, but what I wouldn't give to have a good handful in my fist right now ...

"Yes, you can. I'll email you the transfer paperwork right now. Your supervisor will have to sign off. Do you know when you'd like to start?" she asks.

My supervisor.

Ha.

"Immediately." I sit straighter, reaching for my calculator and punching in numbers, rough calculations of what this move is going to cost me. The number on the screen isn't pretty, but it's a small price to pay if it keeps me from working under him.

"Will do." Sheila chuckles.

I don't.

She wasn't there this morning in the conference room when the entire team gathered for coffee and bagels and the official announcement of who was going to be the new President of Acquisitions for Genesis Financial Securities ... a job for which I was born to do ... a job for which I was told by several people above me was already mine. Unofficially. More or less.

In fact, everyone in the LA office was so convinced I was a shoo-in that only one other person put in for it: a twenty-three-year-old iPhone-addicted former intern who couldn't make coffee unless it came from a Keurig pod or the Starbucks around the corner.

No. Sheila wasn't there when company president Elliot Grosvenor announced in front of all thirty-eight of us that the new head honcho of my department was Reed "Benedict Arnold" York—the man who'd been keeping my bed warm for the past eleven months. The man with whom I'd spent sultry weekends in Napa Valley, sleepless nights in St. Thomas, and sensual summer afternoons in Malibu, hooking up in rooms with sea salt air and ocean views, bonded by our mutual abhorrence for one another while opting not to question our bizarre sexual chemistry. The man who just this morning handed me a little square package wrapped in shiny silver paper with a navy satin bow on top as he said "Merry Christmas" with the strangest look on his face.

I thought it was odd that he'd give me—essentially his fuck buddy—a beautifully wrapped gift, and at first I laughed, thinking it was a joke. But the phone rang, he got called away, and I told him I'd see him at the meeting as he left.

God, I'm an idiot. I really am.

"Joa, please." Reed pushes his voice through my door. He

hasn't budged, and knowing him, he probably won't until I give him some kind of response.

Eleven seconds was all it took to destroy everything we had. To break every unspoken promise he ever made to me. Sure. We weren't dating. But we were exclusive. And he knew how badly I wanted that promotion, how many late nights I'd put in to impress Grosvenor, how many extra projects I'd taken on in an attempt to get noticed. I'd worked more than twice as hard as every other asshole in our department, and Reed was well aware.

"Joa, are you still there?" Sheila asks.

"Yes. Sorry." I clear my calculator and push it to the side of my desk, next to the salted caramel hot cocoa I'd made before the meeting which has since cooled to a tepid room temperature.

The horn section of a Michael Bublé Christmas song blares through the built-in speakers in the ceiling, giving me a quick startle.

"All right, dear. I just sent you the paperwork. We'll have to get a couple sign offs before we can talk official dates, but given that this is a lateral transfer, I don't see why there would be any hiccups. We should be able to get you out there, no problem," she says before waiting a beat. "But I have to ask ... is everything okay? This is so ... out of the blue."

Sheila is sweet to ask, but everyone knows HR's true allegiance is to the company, not the employee. I'm sure the root of her question is based on sniffing out any potential lawsuits or liabilities.

"Everything's fine," I lie. It isn't fine, but it will be as soon as I bid these palm trees adieu. "Just wanting a change of scenery."

"You know, I grew up in Ohio. You couldn't pay me enough to go back to the snow. Those Midwest winters can *be downright brutal." She laughs and sighs at the same time, one of those people who find hilarity in the most mundane of thoughts. "Though you can't beat a white Christmas. Now those I miss."*

I refresh my email and double click on her attachment. An embedded, animated "seasons greetings" image complete with a dancing Santa is displayed at the bottom of the email.

"Printing now," I say. "I'll scan this to you in a few."

I hang up with Sheila, my gaze skimming toward the door where Reed's silhouette still remains. Swiping the papers off my printer, I reach for a logo-emblazoned pen from the logo-emblazoned mug on my desk. When I'm finished, my handwriting is shaky and messy, hardly legible, but my signature is unmistakably on the dotted line and that's all that matters.

I couldn't bring myself to look at him in the boardroom earlier, and the second the meeting was over, I barricaded myself in my office before he had a chance to come at me with some bullshit apology. But now I need to scan this transfer agreement, and that means I'm going to have to open that door and face the man who, just this morning, pulled me into a quiet office corner, pressed his minty mouth against mine, and whispered, "You've got this." An hour later, he texted me to say, "Start thinking of how we're going to celebrate ... ;)"

I clear my throat, rise from my chair, and smooth my palm down the front of my pencil skirt. Can't go over this. Can't go around this. Have to go through this. Grabbing the small stack of papers, I tuck them under one arm and stride across the room to my door. My heart hammers in my ears as I pop the lock, and for a second or two, everything around me spins like I'm on a merry-go-round. If it weren't for the searing and undeniably real tautness in my chest, I might be certain I'm having a nightmare.

Yanking the door open, I find myself blocked by Reed's suited body filling the frame.

"Excuse me." I don't look at him. I look past him.

"Joa." His voice is low, filled with a silent plea, like he wants me to go somewhere with him so we can talk, but what is there to say? What could he possibly say to undo what he's just done?

"Excuse me," I say again, harder.

He still won't move. And to think, once upon a time, I found his gumption charming. Now I know he's a self-serving, arrogant douche who only says and does things to get what he wants. That's not charisma. That's pure ego with a heaping side of self-interest.

Our eyes meet, but only out of habit, not choice.

"I'm sorry," he says, his lips sealing when he's finished speaking. I expected him to have a bevy of excuses and reasons lined up, but apparently the cat has his tongue. Maybe it's better this way. Anything he could say right now wouldn't mean a damn thing. It'd be a waste of perfectly good oxygen and precious time.

Lifting a brow and shrugging a shoulder, I hold his stare. "Okay."

He cups his hand behind his neck, studying me as he massages his tension away. Poor thing. Looks like he's having a terrible day. I have to fight the urge to roll my eyes. I'm a professional, and I won't let some asshat like Reed York get the best of me.

The overhead speakers play some peppy piano-jazz version of Have Yourself a Merry Little Christmas. Such an ironic little soundtrack for this moment.

From the corner of my eye, I spot one of the admins stealing glimpses in our direction, peering out from the bedecked and bedazzled table top Christmas tree on her desk.

I'm sure we're going to be the hot topic with her lunch crew. Everyone knew we were screwing. We tried to hide it at first and then we got lazy, I suppose. All it took was Cara Saunders in Accounting catching Reed's hand grazing my thigh under the table in a meeting last June and the cat was out of the bag, though no one seemed to care all that much since our extracurricular activities never got in the way of our ability to perform our jobs. It was a non-issue.

"Move." I'm done being polite.

Finally, he steps aside, and I make my way to the scanner twenty feet away, fully aware of all the eyes and the heavy, curious stares anchoring me into the carpet. I select Sheila from the list of contacts programmed into the machine and press "scan." Five seconds later, I remove the papers from the feeder tray and return to my office.

He's gone.

And this time next week, I'll be as well.

I refuse to stay here and work under Reed York, to be reminded day in and day out of the man who used my body, toyed with my heart, and stole my promotion right out from under me. He can have the stupid promotion, but he'll never have these lips again. Though who do I think I'm kidding? Obviously, he doesn't care and he never did. He's as fake as LA is sunny. I've lived here just shy of a year, and the one thing I've gleaned so far is that everyone likes to have the appearance of success, the appearance of love, the appearance of wealth, the appearance of being a decent human being. Everyone here is adept at saying the right things at the right time, at moments when they count the most.

But at the end of the day, life here is one big soundstage, complete with carefully selected props and lines and facades.

I want real.

I miss real.

I'm going home.

Next, I buzz my admin.

"Yes, Ms. Jolivet?" Bree answers.

"Cancel my afternoon appointments. I'm taking the rest of the day," I say, packing up my things and shutting down my computer as I mentally compile a moving checklist a mile long. "Actually, I'm taking the rest of the week."

She's quiet, almost as if she's wondering whether or not to pry.

"Enjoy the holidays," I tell her, eyeing the gift on the corner of my desk. "And thanks for everything."

Shoving the shiny silver box with the satin ribbon off my desk, it drops into the waste paper basket with a heavy clunk. It's the last thing I do before locking the door and getting the lights.

10

REED

YOU'VE GOT to be *fucking* kidding me.

My shoes squish against the inch of standing water covering the rented apartment when I get home from Friar Parson's Monday night. I'm assuming a pipe of some kind must have burst in the past few hours, but I'm not sticking around long enough to investigate.

I send a quick text to the owners through the website and throw my things in my bags before scanning through my phone for any other AirBnbs available in the area.

No Results Found.

Of course not. It's the week of Christmas.

Forcing a hard breath through my nose, I pull up another site and search for a hotel, my stomach clenched and a blanket of dread washing over me.

I fucking hate hotels.

But not as much as I hate standing here in cold, wet socks and drenched shoes.

It's slim pickings, but I manage to find a three-star chain option about half a mile from the office.

Grabbing my shit, I lock up and head to the lobby, ordering an Uber on my way.

———

PAM DOES a double-take Tuesday morning when I walk past the front desk. I don't know her, but I'm willing to bet I know what she's thinking: *Reed looks like shit. And he's an hour late.*

The hotel mattress was hard and unsubstantial. The pillows were flat—one of them stained. I promptly called down for a new one, which wasn't delivered for another thirty-seven minutes. And while I tossed and turned most of last night for reasons unrelated to my shitty sleeping accommodations, I woke with the promise of a hot shower.

Only it was lukewarm at best, with bursts of cold.

Typical three-star hotel.

"Good morning," Pam says.

"Yes," I say, heading back to the conference room.

"I have some messages for you," she calls.

I return to her desk and she hands me two scribbled-on sticky notes.

"I didn't think Grosvenor would be up this early," I say, calculating the time difference.

"They were on my voicemail from last night," she says.

"Hello, hello!" A woman in a black, white, and red Christmas sweater carrying a circular tin covered in snowmen bursts through the door. "I'm making my annual cookie run."

A few people step out of their offices and Pam lifts the handset on her phone.

"Joa, your mom's here," she says. "Yes. Okay."

The woman, who's apparently Joa's mother, whips out a stack of paper napkins from her purse and pops the lid off the tin. The sugary scent of Christmas cookies and candies and chocolate-dipped everythings fills the space around us, and people begin diving in like starved vultures.

"I don't think I've ever seen you here before." The woman steps toward me with the same sparkling, baby blue eyes as her daughter and the same slow-and-gentle Liv Tyler cadence to her voice. "I'm Bevin. Joa's mom. And you are?"

"Reed York," I say. "I'm from LA. Just in town for a little while."

"LA? Joa used to work out there. Did the two of you work together?" she asks.

I fight a smirk. Of course Joa wouldn't mention me to her family. Can't say that I blame her.

"We did," I say.

"And what is your role here?" she asks.

"Currently the CFO." And probably not for much longer ...

"Mom." Joa appears out of nowhere, placing her palm on Bevin's shoulder. "I didn't know you were coming by today."

Bevin shrugs. "Your father has an optometrist appointment in the city so I figured I could run these around while he sits in the waiting room. Seemed like more fun than sitting around reading outdated issues of Redbook."

"Oh my God. I'm going to gain ten pounds just looking at these." Kennedy loads a napkin with a stack of treats. "And I'm not even mad about it."

"Enjoy, sweetheart." Bevin laughs before turning back

to us. "So Reed tells me the two of you worked together in LA?"

The color drains from Joa's face, as if she doesn't trust that I kept my mouth shut about our history.

"Briefly," I say. "Which is very unfortunate, because Joa was a priceless asset to our team. We definitely felt that loss."

Joa looks away.

"Well, her father and I were just tickled when she said she wanted to move back home last year," Bevin says. "I think my little adventurer just needed to get LA out of her system."

Little adventurer.

That's funny. I'd have described her the same way. Sexcation after sexcation, she was always up for whatever, never afraid to experience something new, never wanting to revisit the same place.

"You're right, Mom," Joa says, looking at me. "And it's crazy how easy it was to get out of my system once I left."

Touché.

"There's just this toxicity about LA," Joa says. "It's so pretty on the outside, perfect weather, never a shortage of excitement ... but when you get to the heart of it, there's nothing there."

"You don't know LA like I do then," I say, brows meeting.

Two can play this game.

"Pretty sure I got to know LA pretty well while I was there." She squints. "Some might even say too well."

"Can you ever get to know a city too well?" I ask. "Surely you left some parts unchartered. You were barely there a year."

"I saw enough to know I didn't need to see the rest."

Her mother studies us. I'm almost positive Joa forgot she was even standing there.

"I'm so sorry," Bevin says, placing a hand on each of our arms. "I didn't mean to incite such a debate."

"It's not a debate, Mom," Joa says. "Some cities just aren't meant for everyone. I'm sure he feels the same about Chicago."

"I'm actually enjoying Chicago," I say. "In fact, there's nowhere else I'd rather be than right here ... in Chicago."

Her eyes flash and she looks away. "Anyway."

"Have either of you been to Nashville? It's such a beautiful city." Bevin flutters her lashes, her hand over her heart.

Joa and I share a flash of a mutual smile that disappears in half a second—but it's something and I'll take it.

My phone vibrates in my pocket and I excuse myself from the conversation.

"Hello?" I answer.

"Yes, Mr. York? This is Connie at the front desk of the Quality Budget Hotel. We got your request for an upgraded king suite, however, I wanted to let you know that we will unfortunately be unable to accommodate the room change this week. We're at full capacity," the woman says.

My grip tightens. "Then can you get me a mattress that doesn't feel like I'm sleeping on an ironing board?"

The woman laughs, like she thinks I'm kidding.

"I'm being serious," I say under my breath before pinching the bridge of my nose. I can't go another night sleeping like this, let alone another week—or longer depending on how long it takes for me to finish my audit.

"I'm so sorry, sir," she says. "If you'd like, I can send a manager up to inspect your mattress?"

"And if he agrees that it's akin to a piece of cardboard, will he be replacing it?" I ask.

She pauses. "N ... no."

"Then what's the point?"

"Sir ..." The phone muffles for a moment until she returns. "I'm very sorry. If you'd like, I can see if we have any available suites at our sister location in Schaumburg?"

The whole point of me staying at that location is because it's a quick walk to the office.

"That won't be necessary." I end the call, only to turn around and find Bevin still standing there.

"I'm sorry," she says, eyes soft. "I couldn't help but overhear. Are you having issues with your hotel?"

Flattening my lips, I nod. "It's difficult to find a decent place around here on such short notice. All I need is a soft mattress, some clean sheets, and some hot water, but apparently I'm asking too much of this hotel."

"Stay with us."

For a second, I think I heard her wrong.

"We're in Mills Haven," she says. "Joa lives up the street from us. You could stay at our house while you're here and commute back and forth with Joa. I think she takes the L. Hey, Joa ... how long does it take you to get to work?"

Joa's standing by the cookie tin, examining a pretzel covered in chocolate and M&Ms shaped like Rudolph.

"Thirty minutes or so. Why?" she asks.

Bevin turns back to me. "It's no five-star hotel, but it's certainly better than what you're dealing with now."

She has a point.

An extremely valid point.

"That's very kind of you, but I wouldn't feel right imposing," I say. "Especially given that we're two days from Christmas."

"It would be our honor hosting a Genesis executive. The company's been so good to Joa, it's the least we can do," she says. "Do you have plans for Christmas day? Any family in town?"

"No, ma'am. Everyone's back west."

"Then it's settled. You're staying at our house and spending Christmas with us." She's beaming now, hands clasped.

Joa returns to her mother's side. "What are we smiling about?"

"I'm inviting your CFO to stay at our house for the holidays," she says. "I'm not taking no for an answer."

Joa's expression darkens and her eyes narrow. "I'm sure he's fine with his current accommodations. No sense in changing things up when he's already settled."

"Actually, he was just telling me about his hotel and the issues he's been having," Bevin says, twisting the cross pendant around her neck.

Joa lifts a brow. "Hotel? You're staying at a *hotel? You?*"

I sniff. "That's right, Joa. I'm staying at a hotel."

"I told him he could commute back and forth with you," Bevin says to her daughter. "I'm sure the two of you have some catching up to do?"

Joa tries to hide the disappointment on her face from her mother, but I recognize it plain as day.

"It would be nice to catch up," I say, talking to Bevin but looking at Joa. "It's definitely been a while. Though in some ways, it seems like it was only yesterday."

"I have a conference call in ten minutes that I need to prepare for," Joa says. "Thanks for stopping by, Mom."

She leans in, kissing her mother's cheek, and then disappears down the hall into her office.

I gave her space last night at Friar Parson's, because that's what you do when you care about someone and your sheer presence brings out this sadness in their eyes you never knew could exist there.

But I came here to win her back, and I'm running out of time. Besides, I've always been a sore loser.

"So it's settled?" Bevin asks. "You'll stay with us?"

"I'd be honored. Thank you."

PAST

Reed

"Non-work-related question for you." Joa's voice fills the earpiece of my office phone. In the background, I can hear her fingers tapping at her keyboard.

"Yes?"

"You know how we're going to Vail in a few weeks?"

"What about it?"

"I found this really cool resort I think we should look at. I'll send you the link right now."

"Pass."

"You haven't even seen the pictures."

"Resorts are hotels. You know how I feel about hotels," I say, keeping my voice calm and steady.

"Maybe if you told me why you feel the way you feel about hotels, then I'd—"

"Not a chance" The last thing I need is to delve into traumatic childhood memories with the girl who's only with me for the orgasms. "Get back to work, Jolivet."

11

Joa

"LUCY." I force my way into her office the second my mother leaves and all but slam the door.

She ends the call she's on and gifts me with some major side eye and a curious half-leer. "Okay. You're coming at me with some serious ruffled feather energy here. What's going on?"

Ruffled feather energy? That must be one of her mom's trademark terms.

I take the seat across from her, burying my face in my hands for a second.

"What's all this?" Lucy asks. "You're being weird."

"My mom ..." I begin to say, before I break into an incredulous chuckle.

"Oh, no. What'd she do?" Lucy knows all about my mom and her tendencies to go above and beyond when she feels her services are needed in any capacity. She's a born giver. Bevin Jolivet has never met a donation jar she could ignore or a stranded motorist she couldn't stop for. Apparently she places Reed in the same category despite the fact that he could afford the nicest hotel room in town if he wanted and the fact that he chose to spend the holidays alone.

"I guess the apartment Reed was renting flooded or something and he's staying at some hotel that doesn't meet his expectations," I say. "Mom told him he should stay with them."

"No." Lucy's hand flies to her mouth, though I think she's hiding laughter and not shock.

"You think this is funny, don't you?" I ask. "Luc, it's not. I don't want to see him on Christmas. Do you know how weird this is going to be?"

Lucy grabs her phone from her top desk drawer.

"What are you doing?" I ask.

"Calling my mom."

"Why?"

"Because she's one of the best relationship-slash-spiritual gurus in the entire nation, that's why." She holds her phone to her ear. "Hi, Betsy. It's Lucy. Is my mother around? Thanks."

I can't believe she's interrupting her mother's production schedule for this nonsense.

I feel awful.

And at the same time, I'm grateful.

Secretly entertained, too.

"Hi, Mom!" Lucy's face lights as she gives her a condensed version of my ridiculous little predicament, and a moment later, she puts her on speaker and slides her phone across the desk.

"Hi, Dr. Clarke," I say, shooting Lucy a look. I still can't believe she did this. In the year that I've known her, I've only met her mother twice. I doubt she'd so much as remember my face if she passed me on Michigan Avenue.

"Hi, sweetheart," she says, in a voice that makes me feel like I've known her my whole life. Exhaling, my shoulders release their held tension and I focus on the phone in front of me. "So Lucy tells me your ex is in town and your mother has just invited him to stay at your house for the holidays?"

"That's right," I say, thankful this is taking place in the privacy of Lucy's office and not on a production set under hot lights and a live audience. "But my mother doesn't know he and I had a thing … a physical thing … that got ugly in the end. I'm not upset with her for offering—her heart's in the right place. I'm upset with him for accepting the offer."

"Darling, why don't you talk to him about it?" she asks, as if it's the simplest solution in the world. "His boundaries are completely out of line and you have every right to tell him what he did was not okay."

"I could," I say. "But if he changes his mind now, my mom will know something's up and she'll either guilt trip me about it the rest of the week or ask a million questions until she gets enough information to piece together exactly what happened."

She's always been good at that … piecing things together. She'll ask a dozen seemingly unrelated and random questions and then suddenly she's shouting, "YOU SNUCK OUT OF PHOEBE CANTOR'S BASE-MENT TO MAKE OUT WITH JOSH KILDER WHEN YOU WERE SUPPOSED TO BE AT A SLEEPOVER!"

"All right." Dr. Clarke's pregnant pause is concerning. "You know, Joa, in my experience, when life forces us to confront something we've been avoiding it's almost always for the best. It might not seem that way right now, but there's a reason the universe has placed him back in your path."

I offer Lucy a polite smile as I listen to the spiritual side of Dr. Candice Clarke's relationship advice. I've always been much too pragmatic to believe in things like fate and destiny and the universe aligning in the most perfect way at the most perfect time.

"If you don't deal with him now," she continues, "you're going to find him placed in your path again and again until you finally close this chapter of your life."

I suppose she has a point.

I just didn't think I'd be closing the chapter at my childhood home, gathered around my family and a Christmas tree.

"Thank you so much, Dr. Clarke," I say. "I really appreciate the advice."

"Anytime," she says, her voice mellow like a breeze. "Lucy, call me later. Love and light, darlings."

"Bye, Mom." Lucy ends the call and tucks her phone back into her desk drawer. "So? Are we going to do this or are we going to do this?"

━━

REED HAS ALWAYS BEEN two steps ahead of me, though in this case, as we make our way from the L station to my car in the parking lot, he's two steps behind.

We said nothing to each other on the walk to the train, the only sound between us was the rolling of his suitcase wheels against a pitted concrete sidewalk.

Once we got on board, he sat three rows away and on the opposite side—in front of me, even. So I wouldn't have to worry about feeling the burden of his stare on the back of my head for thirty straight minutes.

For most of the day, he left me alone. Tending to his audits and only coming out twice that I noticed.

I don't know what he's planning, only that he's definitely planning something. He's strategic like that. Everything he does is for a reason.

We climb into my car—the same Honda Accord I had in LA, though he always drove us in his Range Rover because growing up in that area, he always knew the best ways to get everywhere, always understood how the time of day correlated with the flow of the traffic.

I start the engine and the radio blares with Rudolph the Red-nosed Reindeer, making me jump in my seat.

Reed laughs.

I crank the volume down and adjust the heat settings.

Heading down Forthwait Street a few minutes later, I can't help but wonder what he's going to think of my parents' home. It's a 1970s split-level that hasn't been updated since they remodeled it in the late nineties. Everything is hunter green and burgundy and oak. It's going to be a far cry from the Malibu manse he grew up in.

At least, I assume he grew up in a Malibu mansion.

He's from Malibu, and he's hinted at his privileged upbringing in the past.

Anyway, it isn't that I care what he's going to think. It's not like I'm trying to impress him. I'm just wondering if he's ever set foot in a house the size of his closet that hasn't aged in almost thirty years.

I almost find it funny, actually.

Every time we'd travel, he'd pick these upscale houses, modern places with pools and art installations and private driveways and landscaping that rivaled paradise.

This couldn't be further from his usual fare.

We round the corner and I pull into my parents' snow-packed driveway, parking beneath the basketball hoop where I beat my brother, Logan, in five straight games of H-O-R-S-E last summer.

It almost feels sacrilegious to have Reed here.

"I'll walk you in," I say, killing the engine.

He climbs out, retrieving his bag from my trunk, and I head toward the garage, typing in my parents' anniversary into the keypad.

The smell of engine oil and frigid garage air hits my lungs and I lead him to the door in case he gets lost in this behemoth.

A moment later, we step inside, wrapped in a hug of indoor warmth.

"Mom? Dad?" I yell.

I know they're home. Both of their cars are here.

"Reed is here," I yell again before climbing the stairs to the next level.

I still can't believe my mom insisted on hosting him this week. Wait. Actually, I can believe it. She doesn't just love to host and entertain, she lives for it. And I'm sure she took one look at Reed, sized him up as a successful, attractive man approximately my age, and thought she could do a little nonchalant match-making.

Reed might be two steps ahead of me, but I'm two steps ahead of my mother.

Making our way through the living room, we pass into the kitchen. The scent of warm, soapy dishwater—a smell I've always associated with home—fills my lungs.

Growing up, my father was a high school math teacher and my mother ran an in-home daycare. Our house always smelled like dish soap, laundry, apple sauce, and Cheerios. I swear the walls of this place practically radiate love and warmth and togetherness.

I can't believe I ever thought I'd be happier in LA than here.

"Mom?" I call for her again.

"Coming!" A second later, she appears from the hallway. "Sorry. Was just putting away some fresh towels in Reed's bathroom. You'll be staying in Joa's old room. She's got a full-sized bed and it's a pillow top, so you should be very comfortable."

"I have no doubt. Thanks again for hosting me," Reed says.

Kiss ass.

"Oh, sweetheart, it's our pleasure," my mother says. "And you know, Tom is just dying to meet you. He's a numbers guy. I assume you are too if you're a CFO. I'm sure you two could talk shop tonight over dinner. I'm making goulash. I hope that's okay?"

Goulash.

I swear my mom makes that every twelve days like clockwork, and she has for as long as I can remember.

Chuckling to myself, I secretly love the fact that he could be eating the finest Chilean sea bass at some Michelin-star restaurant in Chicago tonight, but he's going to be having ghoulash with Tom and Bevin Jolivet instead.

While the two of them are distracted, I sneak out through the front door, climb back into my car, and head to my place.

None of this feels real, and the hazy cast of snow flurries against a dark gray sky only adds to the surrealness.

This is not at all how I pictured any of this going.

PAST

Joa

I stab at my salad with a plastic fork as I sit on bent knees in the middle of Reed's office. I'm in the midst of organizing a presentation, and I wanted to spread out my printed slides so I could visualize them in a fresh way as I prepare my speech.

"Where did you grow up?" I ask after I swallow a bite. When we first started hooking up, I was reluctant to ask him any personal questions, but the more time we've spent together, the more opportunities we've had to reinforce our colleagues-with-benefits-and-nothing-more arrangement still stands. "I don't think you ever told me."

"I'm from the area." He doesn't look up from his computer.

"That could mean anything. Beverly Grove. Culver City. Echo Park. Brentwood ..."

"Malibu."

"Really?" I rest my clear plastic salad container on my

lap. "Wouldn't have guessed that. Did you live by the ocean?"

"I did."

I should've known he came from money. A man who comes from nothing generally doesn't walk with an arrogant swagger like Reed's.

They don't make them like him where I come from. The richest kids in my school were the spawn of doctors and lawyers and bankers. Their homes were beautiful, but they weren't multi-million dollar works of art with breathtaking views.

"Where did you go to school?" I ask.

"Saint Bonne Academy, then Concord Prep, then Pepperdine."

I try to imagine him in a school uniform of khakis and a polo, kissing girls at recess and breaking hearts until the day he graduated a Pepperdine Wave.

"What was it like," I begin to ask, "growing up in a castle by the sea kind of house? Going to all the best schools and having anything you ever wanted at your disposal?"

Reed turns away from his monitor, meeting my inquisitive stare.

"It was awful," he says.

I laugh. "No, really. What was it like?"

"It was awful."

12

REED

QUIETUDE HAUNTS the office on Christmas Eve. Half the staff took the day off. The remaining staff are either checked out, biding their time watching YouTube videos on their phones or pretending to look busy because they're still freaked out that I'm here.

The ride to work this morning was ... interesting.

The train was packed and we were forced to share a seat. On the way home last night, I gave her space. I'm already invading her family on the holidays, it was the least I could do. But today we sat together, the sides of our thighs touching.

She had her nose in a book the entire time—some non-fiction hardback on 18th century women who made a difference or something. Either way, I kept having to adjust myself because there's something so sexy about the way Joa reads.

First, it's the micro expressions. The biting of her lips,

the lifting or furrowing of her brows. Then it's the occasional sigh that I don't even think she realizes she's doing. And don't even get me started on the way she licks the pad of her finger before turning a page.

But most of all, I think it's the fact that she's a well-read, intelligent woman with interests that veer beyond social media and trend-chasing that turns me on the most.

"Pam, why don't you go ahead and order lunch for everyone who came in today," I say, sliding my company credit card across the top of her desk mid-morning. "Anything they want."

Her face lights. I know Harold doesn't treat them to this sort of thing as often as they deserve. He's always kept a clean expense report. No red flags. No superfluous or questionable excesses.

He likes to fly low, stay off the radar.

Little does he know, that little strategy is about to blow up in his smiling face.

Heading back to the conference room, I take a seat, crossing my arms and covering half of my face with one hand as I stare at the piles upon piles of audited reports and evidence, all of them indicating fraud.

Fraud.

Genesis Financial Securities is going down and a lot of good people are going to lose their jobs, but if I don't do anything, a lot of people who trust this place with their hard-earned money are going to lose even more of it.

Gathering a deep breath, I wake my computer and compose an email.

TO: **scott.litchburg@sec.gov**

From: reedyork@gmail.com
Subject: Confirmed

AUDITS FINISHED. **Report to follow.**

———

JOA DROPS me off after work, mumbling something about running home to change and returning in an hour for dinner. Apparently the Jolivets do both Christmas Eve and Christmas Day dinner.

Her father's outside shoveling, his face red and little puffs of cloud-like breath filling the air around him, and he gives his daughter a gloved wave as she backs away.

"Reed," he says as I approach. "How goes it?"

"Great, Mr. Jolivet. Yourself?"

He rests an elbow on top of his shovel handle. "Snow's a bit heavier than I expected. And of course the snow blower's at the repair shop. Going on two weeks now." He shakes his head, and when he speaks he's winded. "But ah, well. Whatcha gonna do?"

"Mind if I?" I point to the red-handled shovel in his hand. There's no sense in him huffing and puffing out here in the cold while I'm loafing in the confines of the warm house he and his wife opened to a complete stranger.

"Oh, you don't have to—"

"I know," I say. "But I want to. I've never shoveled before. We don't get snow back home."

"Right. Well, I suppose I shouldn't deprive you of such an experience." Tom laughs and a second later he's handing the tool over. "Be my guest. Knock 'er off your bucket list."

He supervises me for a few minutes. Or maybe he feels guilty or letting another man do his work. But either way, he doesn't linger long.

Twenty minutes later, the driveway and sidewalk and clear. I dust the snow off my shoulders before heading in through the garage, and I kick my slush-covered shoes off by the back steps. When I head inside, heat wraps me like a blanket. I shrug out of my jacket and place it on a nearby coat rack. And that's when Bevin calls my name, beckoning me to the kitchen where she has a mug waiting for me at the table.

Hot chocolate.

With marshmallows.

And a peppermint candy cane to boot.

———

WE'RE GATHERED around the Jolivet dining table for Christmas Eve dinner. Bevin and Logan ladle and pass out bowls of steaming oyster stew—a decades-old tradition I'm told. Seventies soft-rock style Christmas music plays from a stereo system in the next room, and

"So, Reed," Tom says once Bevin and Logan are settled in their seats. "You worked with Joa in Los Angeles for ... how long was it?"

Bevin swats at his hand. "You know this, Tom. He told us earlier. It was about a year. Isn't that right?"

She looks between the both of us. Joa dips her spoon into her bowl, not making a sound. I nod.

"And were you in the same department?" Tom asks.

"We were," I say. "We worked together pretty closely for a while. Same team and everything."

Joa's gaze darts to mine and she offers the smallest

squint that leads me to believe she's told her parents nothing about me. I figured as much, which was why when her mom served me hot cocoa earlier and nonchalantly grilled me about my love life between questions about my job, I made damn sure not to mention that I'd so much as kissed her daughter before. It wouldn't have taken much for her to put the facts together, I'm certain.

"Now, Joa, you never mentioned that." Bevin points her spoon. "Reed, how long have you been CFO?"

"Not that long. Half a year or so," I say.

"Had you always wanted to climb the corporate ladder, so to speak?" Tom asks.

"No, actually." I answer him, but I look to Joa. "It was never anything I actively sought out. It just sort of ... fell into my lap."

Joa's spoon falls against the lip of her bowl with a loud clang, causing everyone to look her way at the same time.

"This stew is amazing, Bevin." I change the subject for Joa's sake.

Bevin beams. "It's my grandmother's recipe."

"Mom, how does Santa get down the chimney?" One of the twins asks.

"You ask this every day." The other twin smacks her hand across her forehead. "Dad already told you. He shrinks down because he's magic."

Logan stifles a laugh and Tom and Bevin exchange looks.

"That's right," the girls' dad says, pointing at their untouched soups. "And you know he only comes if you eat your Christmas Eve dinner and go to bed on time."

"I'm not hungry." The left twin says.

"Ellison, just try to eat something," Neve pleas. "If you

don't eat, you'll wake up hungry in the middle of the night and if you're up, then Santa won't come."

The other sister kicks Ellison.

"Girls." Their father's voice startles them and they both reach for their spoons at the same time.

The sound of silverware chinking against mismatched china bowls fills the room for a few minutes and the cat won't stop rubbing herself against my ankles.

"I asked Santa for a Barbie Dreamhouse," Ellison announces out of nowhere. She tucks a strand of saffron-colored hair behind her ear and beams proudly at the rest of us. "What did you ask for, Mr. Reed?"

I swallow my bite and buy some time, not expecting to be put on the spot like this.

"Do you think you're on the naughty list or the nice list?" Ellison asks.

Joa arches a brow. I know what she's thinking.

"Nice list," I say, sitting up tall. "Definitely."

"How can you be so sure?" Joa breaks her silence.

"When you do nice things, you make the nice list." I shrug. "It's pretty simple, Joa."

The girls laugh at their silly aunt.

"But what did you ask for?" The one turns her attention to me again.

All eyes have made their way in my direction.

I clear my throat, mulling over the perfect response. If I give some bullshit answer like "forgiveness" or "world peace" it'll make me look trite and go over the girls' heads.

"A Transformer," I say. "Bumblebee."

The twins turn to one another, wrinkling their noses and sticking out their tongues. "Ew. We hate Transformers. We only like Barbies and Shopkins."

"Girls, don't say *hate*." Neve's eyes shift around the

table, but I don't judge. Kids pick up on worse things where I'm from.

"Sorry, Mommy," they say, almost in unison.

"Take a few more bites and then you can play for a little bit." Neve checks her watch. "We'll probably head out in about an hour. Start getting the girls ready for bed."

"Reed, will you play Barbies with us?" Ellison asks.

Joa hides a smirk with her hand, glancing down.

"After we eat," the other sister says. "Will you go to the family room and play Barbies with us? We need someone to be Ken."

Their inquisitive big blue eyes and blonde curls make it nearly impossible for me to turn down their offer, so I take a deep breath and sign my ego away on the dotted line.

"I'd love to," I say.

PAST

Reed

"She's such a kiss ass."

"I know, right? I thought I was the only one who noticed. Glad you see it too."

"I heard she's been screwing with York since she got here."

"Lucky bitch."

"I know. Ever since she got here, he looks at me like I'm about as appetizing as Alpo."

"Is it just me or is her voice really annoying? It's like almost nasally but kind of baby sweet. And she talks so slow. Oh. My. God."

"Yes!"

I clear my throat and step out from behind the breakroom fridge door, a bottle of Fiji water in hand.

Sabrina and Cassidy, two interns who answer phones and file paperwork in HR and who openly aspire to "find rich husbands" after college graduation, whip their little blonde heads in my direction.

"Oh, my God. Reed." Sabrina's hand splays across her chest, her nails painted an annoying shade of glitter bomb aqua. "We didn't know you were standing there."

"You don't say." I keep myself calm so I don't say something I can't take back. The last thing I need is for Frick and Frack to go crying to the head of HR over something I said.

These airheads aren't worth the trouble.

Cassidy can't bring herself to look at me, but I'm getting a bit of a kick out of making them squirm. It's the least I can do after the shit they just spewed about Joa.

Uncapping my water, I linger for a moment, if only to make them squirm that much more.

After a bout of nervous titters and awkward smiles from the two of them, I turn to leave, stopping in the doorway before I go.

"For the record, I'd take Alpo over either of you any day."

13

Joa

I DON'T GET IT.

They love him.

They *all* love him.

Mom. Dad. Neve. Cole. Logan. Emmeline and Ellison. Even the cat, whom I swear is inflicted with some kind of demonic possession, can't stop purring and rubbing herself all over his pant legs.

The family room fireplace crackles and I take a sip of the spiked eggnog in my hand, legs curled up in my chair as I watch Reed play Barbies with the twins in front of the TV.

"No, you be the boy Barbie," Emmeline says, handing him a half-naked Ken. "And I'll be your girlfriend."

"No, I wanted to be his girlfriend!" Ellison says, her little fists balled.

"Maybe we can both be his girlfriend?" Emmeline, our little peacekeeper, suggests.

"You can't have two girlfriends," Ellison says. "Right, Reed?"

Reed watches the two of them fight over him before clearing his throat and lifting the Ken doll to his ear.

"What's that, Ken? You just want to be single right now so you can figure yourself out? That's very mature of you," he says.

I bite my lip, trying not to laugh when I see the way the girls are fascinated with the conversation he's having with Ken.

"What's it mean to figure yourself out?" Emmeline asks.

"It's when you sit back and really think about what you want out of life," he says. "Grown-ups do it all the time."

"Have you ever figured yourself out?" Ellison asks him.

He glances toward me. "I think so, yeah. Closer than I've ever been, anyway."

I stare into the bottom of my empty glass before rising for a refill. Mom and Neve are in the kitchen, making deviled eggs for tomorrow, and Dad and Logan ran out for more firewood.

For the briefest of moments, I almost forgot how angry I was at Reed. Almost forgot the sting of raw betrayal. Sometimes I wonder what would've happened had he not done what he did. Would we be together? Would we be here, right now, just like this?

I still can't believe he was staying at a hotel.

The Reed York I knew was always adamant about never staying at them, though he always refused to tell me why. I never pried because getting him to talk about it was like trying to give a cat a bath. Seemed like it was more work than it was worth.

"How's it going?" Neve asks as I rummage through the fridge. "Reed seems to be keeping the girls busy."

"Yes," I say, letting the fridge close. "Pretty sure the girls don't even know I'm down there. Feeling a little left out."

I wink, refilling my cup.

"It's nice having him here," Mom says. "He makes his bed, picks up his towels, even shoveled the driveway when he got home from work."

"Uh oh. Better be careful. I think we all know where this is going," Neve teases.

Mom elbows my arm, leaning in. "You know, Joa. Reed told me he's single."

I almost choke on my eggnog. "*Mom.*"

"Oh, Mom's been busy getting all kinds of scoop on this one." Neve shoots me a wink.

"No ... just ... please don't make this any worse than it already is," I say.

"Worse than it already is?" Mom's brows knit. She's confused. And rightfully so. She knows nothing, and that's the way it needs to stay.

"It's just awkward, spending the holidays with someone you barely know from the office." I shrug, taking a sip. "That's all."

I walk away before the conversation gets new legs.

Heading down to the family room again, I settle in and grab the remote while the other three are involved in some Barbie drama involving a pink Corvette and a fender bender. Reed, of course, plays the role of the handsome stranger who comes to see if everyone is okay.

Never in a million years would I have imagined Reed York would be hanging out in my parents' house on Christmas Eve playing Barbies with my nieces.

Between this and the hotel thing, I feel like there's a whole other side of him I never knew existed. But he's always been good at throwing curveballs my way, doing things that I least expect him to do.

Kind of like the first time he kissed me.

PAST

Joa

My lips are on fire.

A second ago we were bickering about which Excel graph we should use for our weekly report and then the next thing I knew, his hands were in my hair, my thoughts silenced, and everything around me faded into the background.

"You just ... you just kissed me." I bring my fingertips to my mouth, my narrowing gaze stuck on the man who stole a kiss from me without so much as a warning. "Why? Why did you do that?"

I've only worked here a little over a week, and already I've butted heads with this arrogant Adonis more times than I care to count.

I thought he hated me.

I thought maybe I intimidated him.

But now my ears are ringing and his cinnamon taste is on my tongue.

"Don't go reading into it," he says.

"I thought you hated me."

Reed scoffs. "I don't hate you, Joa. I hardly know you."

"You hardly know me, but you felt comfortable enough to kiss me just now ..."

"You check me out all the time," he says.

I straighten my shoulders as heat flushes my cheeks. He isn't wrong.

"And you get all fidgety when I come around, like you're trying to find a flattering position or something," he continues. "And the other day, you almost walked into that stone pillar by the front desk because you were too busy pretending you weren't trying to pick up the conversation I was having outside Paige's office."

"What's your point? Just because I find you attractive gives you free rein to kiss me?"

"So you admit it. You find me attractive."

"Doesn't everyone? I'm sure you're used to it by now."

Reed drags his palm along his jaw, almost obscuring the vindicated smirk on his face.

"Don't act so smug." I fold my arms before spinning on my heel and heading for the door.

I suppose I shouldn't be all that taken aback by the fact that he kissed me. The tension between us had been building since day one, reaching a fever-pitch intensity just before noon today when we passed each other in the hall and his hand intentionally brushed against mine.

And the looks he gives me during staff meetings, it's like he gets off on watching me squirm under the weight of his stare.

But this? This was a curveball.

"Joa?" he calls after me. I stop, though I don't bother turning to look at him. "You kissed me back."

"I know."
"We should do it again sometime."

14

REED

I'M PERCHED on the edge of a full-sized bed in the middle of Joa's childhood bedroom, accompanied by the glow of a white lace lamp.

The house is quiet—everyone left a half hour ago. They'll be back in the morning, I'm told. They start their Christmas festivities somewhere around nine, though they don't tend to eat until one or so ... says Bevin.

I'm just relieved to get a break from playing Barbies.

As if playing Barbies and doling out Ken-style relationship advice, wasn't awkward enough, Joa insisted on sitting there in a leather recliner, sipping on eggnog and watching the entire thing playing out with this smug look on her face —only moving to refill her drink.

Hope she enjoyed the hell out of that free entertainment. Next time I'm charging.

I grab a framed picture off the nightstand. It's Joa and

her sister, Neve, who's a good five years older than her from my estimate. Joa has braces and glasses and scrawny arms, and they're standing in front of some castle. Disneyland, maybe? I'm not sure. I've never been.

Across the room is a white wicker desk and a bulletin board that hangs over it. Track ribbons and medals are pinned into the canvas with push-pins in various shapes ... hearts, stars, smiley faces, peace signs. A few group pictures are also posted. Track. Dance. Art club.

Debate team—obviously.

From what I gather here and after spending Christmas Eve with her family, it's clear to me that Joa had a happy, All-American childhood—one of the things I'd have given anything for when I was a kid.

While the Jolivets will never know this, they gave me quite the gift tonight. To be a part of something I've only ever seen on TV or in the movies means more to me than they could begin to comprehend.

I tug my shirt over my head and glance at my vibrating phone on the quilt. The screen lights with a picture from Bijou.

I tap the message, a photo of her with a few friends, drinking out of festive glasses and wearing headbands with what appear to be blinking Christmas lights.

"Wish you were here!" she writes.

Good to know she's having fun and not sitting at home throwing herself a pity party.

She doesn't ask what I'm doing tonight, and that's fine. If I told her I spent the evening with a family who wears ugly Christmas sweaters, Santa hats, and holds holiday-themed karaoke contests, she wouldn't believe me. And if she did, she'd give me shit. We might share the same DNA, but we're cut from two completely different cloths.

But I don't care. I wouldn't want to spend the holidays anywhere else or with anyone else.

PAST

Reed

"Trust me, York. I know what I'm talking about. I wrote a paper on this two years ago." She leans over my desk on a scorching July afternoon, jabbing her pointer finger against a stack of paper. *"The Coswell Growth and Projection Model is by far the most accurate out there when it comes to cryptocurrency. I don't feel comfortable using any other method, not with our clients."*

"The Greenleaf Model is newer, and they've incorporated Ripple and Dogecoin and Stellar's historical data into their algo."

"Dogecoin and Stellar are irrelevant," she says. *"They're ants compared to us. Their data is useless, and we'd be doing our clients a huge disservice by soiling their projections with inaccurate data."*

God, I love it when she uses big words.

"Let it go," she says, straightening her shoulders. *"If you*

want to go rounds, we can go rounds. I was the debate team captain all four years of high school, and I took us to state."

"Not the least bit surprised by that."

"So you can surrender now or we can keep going. It's your choice." Her right hand flies to her hip. "Why are you laughing? What's so funny?"

"You." I rise from my desk, straighten my tie, and make my way to the other side where she stands with planted heels, her body terse. "Your passion, your intelligence... it's sexy as hell ..." leaning in, I whisper, "You have no idea how hard I am right now."

I manage to get a smile out of her.

"I think we need to plan on staying late tonight," I say. "These projection model reports aren't going to run themselves."

15

Joa

FOUR PIES ARE STACKED in my arms as I make my way up the front steps to my parents' house, each step as careful as the one before. The moment I make it over the threshold, I'll have to see him again.

It's bad enough he was the last thing I thought about before I went to bed and the first thing I thought about the second I woke up this morning. Now I have to spend the entire day with him, "making merry" because it's Christmas.

I scolded myself this morning. Silently, of course.

I thought I was stronger than this. I was one-million percent sure I'd be able to resist his charms, that he wouldn't be able to weasel his way into my good graces. But watching him play so sweetly with my nieces last night nearly melted the ice from my heart, and hearing how he shoveled the driveway for my dad chipped away at my resolve a little bit.

The Reed York that I knew wouldn't have done those

things. He wasn't generous, polite, or well-mannered. He was entitled and selfish and distant.

Now I'm thinking there's so much more to him than I ever imagined—not that it matters. And not that it changes anything. He did what he did. There's no taking away from that. No going back. No undoing the damage.

I show myself in and latch the door behind me, carrying the pies up to the kitchen where my mom is lining potatoes up next to the sink as she hums Little Drummer Boy.

She doesn't see me until I shrug out of my coat and yank my woolen cap off my head.

"Oh, Joa," she says, clutching at her heart. "When did you get here?"

"Just now." I stride over to her, throwing my arms around her shoulders from behind and breathing in the familiar scent of her Liz Taylor perfume and Redken hairspray. "Brought four pies. Hope that's enough."

"As long as we don't have four slices each, it should be plenty," she says with a chuckle. "Though you never know with Logan. That man can put down two large pepperoni pizzas and still complain about being hungry an hour later."

"Some things never change." I grab a spare potato peeler from the drawer and take the spot beside her at the sink.

It's quiet for a few moments. The metallic slink of the peeler, the steady stream of the water, the quiet thunks of the peelings landing against stainless steel.

"You know," Mom says, breaking the silence. "That Reed is a very nice man."

I want to roll my eyes. I know exactly where this conversation is headed.

"Yeah, sure," I say, not wanting to have a disagreement with my mother the morning of Christmas.

"And I can tell, he really thinks the world of you," she continues.

I'm sure anything he's saying is out of politeness. "I bet he does."

"I guess I just don't understand the indifference."

I turn to her. "Mom."

"No, seriously, Joa. He's smart and handsome and successful, and don't think I don't notice him stealing glances at you every chance he gets."

I laugh, reaching for another potato and running it under the stream of water.

"That ship has sailed," I say, opting not to go into detail.

"Did the two of you date? When you were in LA?"

"No." It's not a lie. "We never dated."

"Well, all I'm saying is to give him a chance. We all think he's very nice." She grabs a potato.

"Didn't anyone tell you?" I ask. "Nice boys went extinct a good decade ago."

"Logan's a nice boy." She shrugs.

"Logan's not a boy. He's a thirty-five-year-old manchild," I say, though manwhore might be more fitting. "And you have to say he's nice. You're his mother."

"So my opinion doesn't count because I gave birth to him?"

"Exactly."

"Joa Marie." Mom shakes her head, rinsing a spot of dirt off her hand.

"What?"

"Would it be so bad if you just … gave him a chance?" she asks. "When the two of you worked together, did he ever flirt with you or anything?"

I almost choke on my spit. "There was some flirting, sure."

She nudges me with her elbow. "See."

"See *what*?" I ask.

"You two have chemistry."

I steady my hands on the edge of the sink, pulling in a ragged breath. I so badly want to blurt out, "He stole that promotion from me," but I don't want to ruin Christmas by shattering her warped perception of him.

"He's nice to look at," I say. "And maybe once I thought I could see myself dating him ... but trust me when I say, the two of us together would never work. Once you get beyond that annoyingly perfect exterior, there's not much there to work with. He's just as vain and vapid as the rest of them."

I'm going to hell.

I've never spoken such mean words about anyone in my entire life—not even him—but I need my mom to drop it.

Reaching for another potato, I stop when the familiar scent of Reed's Creed cologne fills the space around us.

"Good morning, Joa," he says.

I turn to face him, my heart in my teeth. His hair is damp from the shower, his eyes search mine. There's a hint of sadness in the way he looks at me, an emotion I never knew he was capable of feeling.

He heard.

He heard everything.

"Sleep well?" my mother asks, lashes batting.

Reed nods. "I did. Thank you. Let me know if you need any help with anything."

His voice is terse, his jaw set. He turns to leave. I don't know where he's going, but I can see his anger in the tightness of his shoulders.

"Fix this," my mom whispers.

Wiping my wet hands on a dishtowel, I go after him. I should apologize. I feel awful, I do.

"Reed," I say, stopping him between the living room and the hall to the bedrooms. "Wait."

He turns to me and says nothing.

"I'm sorry," I say.

Still, he doesn't speak.

Hooking my hand around the bend of his elbow, I pull him into my room so we can speak in private.

"I didn't mean it," I say, "I was just—"

"—of course you did," he cuts me off. "But that's okay, Joa. Call me vain and vapid all you want. I've been called worse."

His demeanor is solid, iron-like and serious, and his gaze pierces mine.

Parting my lips, I begin to respond until he silences me with a kiss.

His hand cups the side of my face, his thumb bracing the underside of my jaw and his fingers slide into my hair.

The kiss is soft and gentle and earth-shattering at the same time. I feel it everywhere. In the goosebumps on my flesh. In the empty cavities formerly known as my lungs. In the runaway gallop of my heart.

Heat passes from his lips to mine, and I breathe it all in —the bittersweetness of this moment, the hurt, the anger, the longing ... *him.*

And then I push him away.

Our eyes meet, his are wild, desperate almost. I've never seen this side of him, and I couldn't look away if I tried.

"I've failed you, Joa. I know that," he says. "In more ways than one. And I can forgive your harsh words. But I can't forgive the fact that you stand there and you continue to deny that I'm the only man who's ever going to be right for you and you're the only woman who's ever going to be right for me."

I fold my arms across my chest, looking out my old bedroom window. "What am I supposed to do with that, Reed? Huh? What am I supposed to do with that? You didn't just betray me. You *blindsided* me."

"I didn't have a choice."

My gaze flicks to his. "Bullshit."

His left hand rests on his hip and the indentation below his cheekbone hollows.

I move toward the door, stopping before I leave. "All you had to tell them was no."

PAST

Joa

I'm staring at the ceiling from a plush top king-sized bed in some one's Newport Beach vacation rental when an email pings my phone.

I'd turned on my alerts before we got here, knowing that HR was going to let me know if I made the cut for the final rounds of interviews for the VP of Acquisitions position.

Madeleine retired months ago, but for reasons unknown, they're taking their sweet time filling her spot. That tells me either they already know who they want and they're biding their time ... or they're trying not to rush the process so they can examine each and every candidate until they find the best fit.

From what I've heard, only a couple of other people from the office applied. The rest of the applicants have been from outside the corporation.

I don't want to get my hopes up, but I feel like the odds are in my favor.

Reed is in the kitchen, grabbing a slice of cold pizza from the fridge. He hates it when I look at my phone in bed, swears the glow of the screen keeps him awake even when I've turned the brightness all the way down, so I grab my phone from the nightstand and tap my inbox, hoping I can read my email before he gets back.

Traffic was a bitch on the way here this afternoon, and Grosvenor was on Reed's case all morning about delays with some contract he'd been working on.

Needless to say, he's in a mood tonight.

To: joajolivet@genesisfinancialsecurities.com
From: HR@genesisfinancialsecurities.com

Dear Joa,

We are pleased to inform you that you have been selected as a finalist for the Vice President of Acquisitions position.

Your next interview will be Thursday at nine o'clock.

Please let us know if that time does not work for you.

Sincerely,

Paulette Duncan

Director, Human Resources
Genesis Financial Securities

"You're smiling." Reed stands in the doorway holding a paper plate piled with stale slices of pepperoni and green pepper pizza.

"Am I not allowed to smile?" I tease.

"Here." He hands me a slice of cold pizza.

"How sweet of you."

"I try."

"I got the email," I say. He knows exactly which email I'm referring to. He's only heard me talk about it every day for months.

He chews, swallows. "And?"

The muted TV flickers to the side of him, playing an Office rerun—the one where Andy proposes to Angela at Toby's going away party.

"I'm a finalist." I try to keep my exterior cool and collected but on the inside, I'm screaming. The inside me is begging me to pull a Tom Cruise and jumping on this bed.

"Are you serious?" he asks before taking a seat on the edge of the bed next to me. "Joa, that's ... that's incredible. You'd be perfect for that position."

His words are encouraging and he wears a smile, but it doesn't reach his eyes.

Did he secretly want the job?

Or is he worried about how it's going to be if I get the job and I'm no longer working side by side with him, sharing those late nights and stolen moments.

"You weren't interested in the job, were you?" I ask.

"God, no. Working side by side with Grosvenor is a fate worse than hell," he says. "But I'm sure you'll do just fine."

I laugh through my nose.

"Can't think of anyone else more perfect for the job," he adds. "You're exactly what they like. Intelligent, diligent, and still green enough that they can mold you into the kind of VP they want you to be."

I know he isn't wrong. They might try to mold me to an extent, but if they think I'm going to be some finger-puppet, then they're mistaken.

"You swear you don't want the job?" I ask, studying him in the dark of the bedroom.

"Trust me," he says. "I don't want the job."

16

REED

WE'RE SEPARATED by two flickering red candles of differing heights and a plethora of mismatched dishware, but there might as well be an ocean between us.

The twins pick at their food, both of them appear to be going for the all-carb diet with plates full of rolls, scalloped corn, and mashed potatoes.

Neve gave them each a little scoop of green bean casserole, which prompted them both to stick their tongues out, and Cole muttered something under his breath about how "at least they're eating *something*."

The scalloped corn is making its way around again, and I help myself to another serving. I've never seen so much comfort food in one place in my life. In fact, I can't say that I've ever eaten a casserole for a holiday dinner.

Today's full of all kinds of firsts—including the first time I kissed Joa in over a year.

Her attention has been laser focused on her plate for the past twenty minutes. She hasn't looked up at me once.

Tom and Cole are seated down at the end of the table, waxing poetic about the Bears while Neve and Logan and Bevin discuss the logistics of some upcoming family reunion in Napersville.

The girls are busy shoving bread in their faces.

That just leaves us.

Our silence is obvious, though her family is the polite kind, the kind that doesn't draw attention to the kinds of things that might make others uncomfortable.

If my sister were here, she'd have said something five minutes into the radio silence. She didn't come equipped with a filter, that one.

In a few days' time, I'll be able to tell her everything.

Until then, I just need to bide my time and try not to make anything between us more strained than it already is.

"So, Reed, what might your family be doing tonight?" Bevin asks, dabbing the corners of her mouth with a holly-green paper napkin before reaching for her mulled cider.

"Probably sitting on a beach somewhere on the other side of the globe, drinking Mai Tais and trying to remember what day it is." I reach for my beer. A couple of them laugh until they realize I'm not joking.

"No family traditions, I take it?" Tom asks.

Shaking my head, I take a sip. "That's never been our thing."

Correction—it's never been Bebe and Redford York's thing.

"Do you have any brothers or sisters or is it just you?" Neve asks.

"I have a sister. Her name is Bijou and she's a few years younger," I say.

"You two don't spend the holidays together?" Joa's dad asks.

"Depends on the year. Depends on our schedules." I realize that I'm implying that I spend the holidays alone. I've never admitted that before. Not out loud anyway. I feel the heaviness of Joa's gaze, but by the time I glance up, she looks away. "My family ... we're nothing like *this*."

"Well that's perfectly fine, Reed," Bevin says, lifting her glass and pointing it at me. "Every family is different. There's no right or wrong way to celebrate—or not celebrate."

"I find it fascinating." Neve rests her chin on top of her hand, her elbow on the table. That would never fly at my house growing up—yet another thing I'm growing to love about this family. They're laid back. No one's fussing at anyone else about using the proper silverware. No one changes for dinner. There's no superficial stuffiness in the air.

"Fascinating how?" Joa's brother asks.

Neve turns to him and shrugs. "Just how his family does their own thing for the holidays. Can you imagine if Mom and Dad booked a trip to Tahiti or something and left us to fend for ourselves?"

Logan sniffs. "That's a little insensitive, don't you think?"

Neve's eyes dart to mine. "I don't mean it that way."

"I know," I say.

"I just can't wrap my head around spending the holidays alone," she says. "I know you're used to it, but that has to be hard sometimes, right?"

"Neve," Joa speaks up.

"It isn't hard when it's the only thing you've known," I

say. "I don't think we've spent a Christmas together since I was maybe eight or nine?"

"You're joking." Neve's mouth is agape. "What'd you do Christmas morning? Who was there when you opened presents?"

My left palm digs into my thigh under the table and the collar of my shirt rubs against my heated neck. This feels like a therapy session now. Or an incredibly invasive date—the kind where I'd normally excuse myself to "take a call" and then get the hell out of there.

"Usually one of the nannies." I answer Neve, despite the fact that I know how this sounds. Poor little rich boy. Taking another swig of beer, I smile at the Jolivets. "Can't choose your family, am I right?"

I steal a look across the table, catching Joa's stare. Only this time she doesn't look away. She sits there, unmoving, though she isn't nibbling the inner corner of her bottom lip while appearing lost in thought. It's as if she's studying me, seeing me for the first time—again.

"Mama, can I go watch Frosty the Snowman?" One of the twins breaks the silence and suddenly people are moving and shuffling and breathing and eating and drinking again. "Grandpa said he taped it for me on the DVR."

"Yes, sweetheart. That's fine," Neve says, eyeing her untouched plate but not saying a word. They say in life you have to choose your battles. I imagine that applies with six-year-olds as well.

One little tow-headed girl dashes into the next room, followed by the other. A minute later, the sound of the TV blares over the stereo system, drowning out Nat King Cole.

"Turn it down, Ellison," Neve yells from the table—yet another thing that wouldn't have flown at my house growing up.

Nat King Cole's velvet tenor returns and the cartoon sounds fade into the background. Neve and her husband chuckle and Bevin smiles, placing her hand over her heart. She's textbook grandma sweet. She finds anything and everything the twins do endearing and adorable.

I never met my mother's mother. She passed before I was born. But my father's mother was something else. She was obsessed with me, intentionally going out of her way to make Bijou feel inferior any chance she got. One year she gave me a hundred-dollar bill in a Christmas card as well as the newest PlayStation console. At the same time, she gave Bijou a pack of stickers with the cellophane already torn. Bij was only seven but she was old enough to know the difference between our gifts. As the years passed, the more Grandma Constance showered me with riches and spoiled me with attention, the more I pushed her away, doing my best to act like a spoiled, ungrateful brat of a grandson so she would stop with the lopsided affections. It wasn't fair to my sister.

I mentioned it to my parents once and they shrugged it off, saying that's how she's always been and they had no intentions of doing anything other than sweeping it under the rug.

"*She doesn't do well with other females. Believe me, I speak from experience,*" my mother had said. "*We just ignore it. She won't be around forever ...*"

And she wasn't.

She passed when I was thirteen, proving that just because you're heartless doesn't make you insusceptible to heart attacks.

My parents missed the funeral, unwilling to interrupt their Bali vacation. Instead they sent flowers and mentioned something about holding a private memorial service when they returned—which never happened.

By the time dinner is over, half the crew scatters to the family room. I grab a few dishes and carry them to the kitchen, placing them in a stack by the sink.

Growing up, I never had chores—though it didn't stop me from asking for some.

"Darling, that's why we have help," my mother would say with a silly laugh as she pressed her finger against my nose.

"The meal was amazing, Bevin. Mind if I wash the dishes?" I ask her when she places another stack beside mine. I realize it's an odd request. I just don't know if I'll ever get a chance to do something like this ever again. Washing my own dishes isn't the same.

Bevin laughs. "Do I mind? Goodness, no. They're all yours. The Palmolive's under the sink."

I fill one half of the sink with warm, soapy water that smells like sweet apples, grab a soft sponge, and get to work.

Neve and Joa bring a few more dishes my way before Bevin shoos them away.

"You wash, I'll dry?" she asks, grabbing a clean towel from a drawer.

"Sure."

"I hope you're enjoying yourself today," she says when I hand her a plate. "I know it can be hard, spending Christmas with a bunch of weirdos like us."

I chuckle. "It's fine. And I'm glad to be here. You have a lovely family."

She nods, pausing. "I hope you weren't offended by Joa's comments earlier. I think I backed her into a bit of a corner. I do that sometimes. She was only saying it because—"

"—no need to worry. We had a chat. Cleared it up," I say.

From the corner of my eye, I watch her crack a smile. "Oh, good. Glad to hear that."

I hand her a shiny, dripping wet fork.

"She's always been my restless soul," Bevin says, polishing the tines. "Doesn't know what she wants or how she feels half the time. Scared of making real decisions, you know? She's a bit complicated, that one."

I dunk another plate in the water. "Aren't we all?"

PAST

Reed

I stand outside Grosvenor's office at a quarter to nine on a tepid December morning. He buzzed me and asked me to meet him for a quick chat about the Wellesley account a little while ago, only from out here I can hear that he's stuck on a phone call.

Leaning against the wood-paneled walls, I check my phone, aimlessly scrolling, mindlessly reading—until I hear him say Joa's name.

"She's perfect," he says. "She'll be our fall guy ... She's desperate for the job and eager to please and she'll do anything I tell her to do ... right ... I know ... I think so too ... I'm about to make the announcement in a half hour ... sounds good, Harold. Yep ... later."

My blood runs ice cold as I process what I just heard—or rather what I think I just heard.

So Joa got the job—but he's setting her up?

For what?

I knew Grosvenor was a slimy bastard from the moment we met, but I never imagined he'd stoop this low.

Knocking on his door, I wait.

"Come in," he calls a second later. Grosvenor sits up straight in his throne-sized chair when he sees me. "Reed. Hi."

I place the files on his desk, jaw clenched as I try to steady my breathing.

"Sir, before we dive into the Wellesley account, I wanted to let you know that I've given more thought to your offer," I say, referring to the half dozen or so times he's pulled me aside over the past few months, all but offering the VP position to me on a shiny silver platter.

Each time, the salary would grow, the benefits package would have a couple of extra goodies thrown in, and he'd carry on about what an asset I am to the company and how he's had me in mind for the job since before Madeleine announced her retirement.

There may have been a time when I wanted the job just as badly, but that was before Joa came along and proved her worth. And when she told me she'd put in for the job, I didn't bother wasting my time. I knew if I applied, I'd get it. No question. And I couldn't do that to her.

But now, it would appear that I don't have a choice.

She's being set up, and I'll be damned if I stand back and let it happen.

Sure, I could let her take the job and tell her what I heard, but if we're going to figure out what the hell's going on, we need someone Grosvenor knows and trusts.

Someone who's been to his house.

Someone he treats better than he does his own son.

Someone he thinks the world of.

Me.

"All right, Reed," Grosvenor says, elbows resting on his desktop and hands folded. "And what have you decided?"

"I'd like to accept the position." My stomach tightens. She's going to hate me for this. "If it's still available."

Grosvenor's thin lips stretch wide and he slaps the desk. "Way to pull through at zero hour, Reed. But I never lost hope. I figured you'd come to your senses."

His excitement stretches from his eyes to his dancing fingertips. He seems all too eager to make me his fall guy, but maybe his reasons are simple in nature. Maybe they mirror the very same reasons I think I'm better equipped to get to the bottom of whatever little plan he's hatching.

He thinks I trust him.

———

The last thing I expect when I call the SEC tip line is to be placed in touch with a live human.

"Scott Litchburg, Enforcement Division, how can I help you?" the man on the other end answers.

I'm sitting in the driver's seat of my Range Rover in a quiet corner of an underground parking garage. It was about as far away as I could get without leaving the place completely, and I can't be gone long. The staff meeting is in a half hour and he's going to make the announcement then.

I tell Scott what I know, which isn't much, but he agrees that it's worth looking into. He asks me a few more questions, apologizing for the periodic silence on his end as he jots them down with pen and paper, and then he collects my contact information.

"Oh, and Mr. York, one more thing," Scott says before he ends the call. "This is officially an active investigation—case number d-as-in-dog, x-as-in-x-ray, four, six, eight, one, one, *two, one. All evidence and information—no matter how big or inconsequential you believe it to be—is property of the Securities and Exchange Commission's Enforcement Division and is hereby declared confidential. Any violation thereof is punishable by a fine of up to—but not to exceed—one million dollars as well as up to ten years' imprisonment."*

He sounds like he's reading off a script.

"I just need to make sure we have an understanding," he says. "You can't tell your Mama or your wife or your girlfriend or your dog. I don't care if you trust them with your life. This is federal property and cannot be shared with anyone outside of this investigation until this file is closed. Do you understand, sir?"

"I understand." I bury my head in my left hand, my fingertips digging into my pulsing temples.

I won't be able to warn Joa.

I won't be able to tell her a damn thing for who knows how long.

I hang up with Litchburg and check the time.

The meeting starts in five minutes. It'll take me that long just to get back up to the eighth-floor conference room.

Heading back, there's only one thing on my mind. And when I make it to the meeting with thirty seconds to spare, that thing flashes me the prettiest smile that fucking obliterates my heart—though not nearly as much as I'm about to obliterate hers.

Just this morning I kissed her and told her the job was in the bag, that there was no way they'd pass her up.

I wished her good luck.

And then I handed her a little silver box with a blue ribbon containing a gift that will be absolutely nothing the second Grosvenor makes his announcement.

"All right, folks. Let's get to it. I know it's Friday so I'm going to make this quick and painless. Just one announcement for you today," the man of the hour strides in and takes his place at the head of the conference room table, a leather folio pad under his arm and a cup of coffee in his hand. How he can be so casual while simultaneously hatching some kind of scheme sends a flash of red to my vision that disappears when I feel a kick under the table.

Glancing up at Joa, who's seated across from me, she mouths the words, "I'm so nervous" and then pretends to do a silent scream, her little fists clenched.

She's looking for reassurance.

"As you know, we've been without a VP of Acquisitions for the better part of the year, and I know we're all anxious to get someone in there." He pauses to take a drink from his mug. "I'm happy to let you know that we've extended an offer to someone—and as of this morning, that someone has accepted."

From my periphery, I catch Joa's gaze snapping to me—not because she knows, but because she's confused.

"Reed, if you'd stand up please." Grosvenor points to me. "Everyone, you're looking at the new Vice President of Acquisitions."

I steal a glance at Joa while the room erupts in stilted, forced applause. I think they're all just as confused as she is.

Her eyes water and her chest rises, but it doesn't fall.

She's holding her breath, holding it in.

Waiting until she can be somewhere far from me, I'm sure.

"Reed, again, congrats," Grosvenor says, "Everyone else, back to work."

He laughs because he's exactly the kind of man who finds himself hilarious, and everyone begins to shuffle out.

Joa won't look at me and I can't blame her.

She squeezes between a handful of people, slipping out the door before I get the chance to catch up.

When I get to her office, the door is locked.

"Open the door, Joa," I say, keeping my voice low but still loud enough that she can hear me. "Joa, please."

She ignores me, but I wait, undeterred by the fact that I'm the last person she wants to see right now and also by the fact that I can't give her an explanation.

With hands splayed wide against the frame of her door, I ignore the curious stares I get when people pass and I wait.

And wait.

Until the door is yanked open.

I don't move.

"Excuse me," she says, refusing to look at me.

"Joa." There's nothing I can say, but maybe it won't matter what I do or don't say but how I say it.

She's known me for almost a year now, and honestly, she probably knows me better than anyone.

If she would just look at me, she would know that I never meant to hurt her.

"Excuse me." Her voice is harder this time, though it does little to mask the quiver in her words.

For the smallest moment, our stares catch, and I use the opportunity to say, "I'm sorry."

"Okay." She shrugs, indifferent.

I deserve that.

I hook my hand behind my neck, watching her stand there with a small stack of papers clenched against her chest as she eyes the scanner in the common area outside her office.

"Move," she says.

I step aside and let her through, watching as she scans her papers.

Space.

I'll give her some space.

She needs to cool down so we can have a rational conversation about this.

Returning to my office, I close the door, close my eyes, and close the chapter of a book I was far from close to finishing.

By the time I come out a few hours later, I pass her darkened office.

She must have taken the afternoon.

I let myself in, surprised at the fact that she left it unlocked, and sit at her desk, ripping a Post-It from a cube beneath her monitor and grabbing a pen from her top drawer. Only before I have a chance to scribble a note to her, something catches my eye.

The silver box with the blue ribbon rests neatly on top of the trash can.

I leave a note with a single sentence: "It's not what you think."

If I can pique her curiosity come Monday, after she's had a chance to cool off, maybe I can salvage this.

Retrieving the gift from the garbage, I carry it back to my office. By the time I arrive, I've already checked out, opting to give myself the rest of today, but a flashing red light on my phone and a voice mail from Grosvenor have other plans for me.

17

Joa

HE HAS A SUITCASE.

And he's hugging my mother.

I pull into my parents' driveway the Friday after Christmas to pick Reed up for our AM commute, only I wasn't expecting him to bring his baggage along for the ride.

I press the trunk release, grip the steering wheel with a gloved hand, and wait for him to load up and get inside. Mom watches from the front step, wrapped in her fuzzy robe, a snowman mug in her left hand. I give her a small wave and she nods. Is she ... is she *teary-eyed*?

"Morning," I say a minute later as Reed buckles up.

"Morning."

"Are you going home today?" I ask, shifting into reverse.

"No."

"Decide to give that hotel another shot?" I ask.

"No."

"You found another AirBnb?"

He checks his phone. "I did."

I want to ask if this has anything to do with what I said yesterday, but I don't want to go down that road again. There's no point in dredging up a stale conversation that's only going to lead to nowhere.

I turn toward the train station just as he takes a phone call. He says a few words like, "Yes ... okay ... today ... later." And then he ends the call.

"What are you auditing anyway?" I ask as I pull into the parking lot.

"Not at liberty to say at this time," he says, spoken like a true corporate finger puppet.

He never used to be this way.

He was casually arrogant, laidback, a good-time guy on his best of days and an infuriatingly sexy prick on his worst of days. But it was always something I could roll with.

This ... I can't.

We don't speak for another ten minutes. And it's only when we've settled into a shared bench on the train that he leans in and says, "You have a very lovely family, Joa. You're extremely lucky."

I don't know what to say to that other than, "Thanks."

The next few minutes are filled with track noise, people coughing, someone talking on their phone several notches too loud.

"Reed?" I ask.

He looks up from his phone. "Yes?"

There are a thousand things I could ask him right now, but in this moment, I only have one. "What's your thing with hotels? Why do you hate them so much?"

He pulls in a slow breath, his chest rising beneath his black woolen coat, and then he stares ahead at the seatback in front of him, this blank look on his face. When I look to his lap, I notice the whites of his knuckles as he holds his phone too tight.

I'm seconds from telling him he doesn't have to answer, when he begins to speak.

"My parents used to leave me alone in hotel rooms," he says. "Hours at a time, sometimes sun up to sun down. I was probably three or four the first time. Or maybe that's the first time I was old enough to realize what was going on. They'd just plop me in front of a TV and point me toward the snacks in the mini bar."

For a moment, I think he's kidding. I can't imagine millionaires taking exotic vacations and being so careless with their precious cargo. I'd expect that kind of behavior from someone strung out on meth—not from a glamourous couple living the high life in the upper echelon of society.

"My god, Reed." I lift my fingers to my mouth, horrified. "You mentioned before that you had nannies growing up. Your parents didn't bring them along?"

"The nannies came along after Bijou was born. Apparently it was a status symbol in my mother's circle back then to *not* have a nanny," he says. "To prove that you could do it all. But when my sister arrived, my mother threw up her white flag and hired an entire team to handle the two of us."

"I'm so sorry." I'm not sure what else I can say. I can't imagine how that must have been for him as a small child. He must have been terrified. No wonder he avoids hotel rooms now—they're tiny prison cells, and he doesn't want to feel that abandonment all over again.

My heart softens for him—for the little boy he once was and for the kind of grown man he never got a chance to become.

Everything makes sense now—the heartlessness. The callousness. The selfishness.

It's how he was raised.

The rest of our commute is silent.

When I get to work, I'll text my mom and ask if she knows anything, and then I'll pray she doesn't read into my curiosity, call me, and then keep me on the phone for twenty-six minutes trying to convince me to give him a chance.

Locking myself in my office, I text my mom and fire up my computer. My emails load, and I glance up at the screen, half scanning the senders as they populate, but it's the last one that catches my eye.

An email from our Manhattan branch sits at the top of my inbox with a little red exclamation point beside it.

My heart races.

A month ago, on a whim, I'd applied for a temporary position out there, filling in for one of the division coordinators while she took a twelve-week maternity leave. I was in a funk, craving a change of scenery, a change of routine. a bit of an adventure, and I've never lived in New York.

TO: **joa.jolivet@genesisfinancialsecurities.com**
**From:
ian.iaconelli@genesisfinancialsecurities.com**
Subject: Manhattan Offer

JOA,

I hope this email finds you well and that you enjoyed the holidays with your family in Chicago.

I wanted to touch base with you regarding

your interest in filling in for Jolene while she goes on maternity leave next month.

As it turns out, Jolene has decided not to return once she has the baby, so we are looking for a permanent replacement.

I've spoken to Harold and reviewed your accounts and I think you'd be a great fit for our Manhattan team, not to mention this position is a stepping stone to senior management in the long-term if that's something that interests you.

If you're interested in accepting my offer, please give me a call at your earliest convenience.

I hope to hear from you, Joa.

RESPECTFULLY,
Ian Iaconelli

Manhattan Branch Manager
Genesis Financial Securities

BEFORE I HAVE a chance to read it a second time, my office phone rings.

"Yes, Pam?" I answer.

"Your mother is on line two," she says.

I press the two key and hope we can keep this brief. Love her to pieces, but I think she forgets that not everyone is retired and has all the time in the world to chit-chat.

"Hi, Mom," I say.

"Joa," she says. "I got your text message ... the one about Reed."

"So what's going on? Why did he leave?" I ask.

"He just said a place came open over by the office, and he felt bad imposing. I told him he wasn't imposing at all, but he said he'd already paid or something."

I wait for her to continue with her story, but there's nothing more.

"That's it?" I ask.

"That's it."

"He didn't say anything else?" I ask.

"Oh. You're wanting to know if this has to do with you," she says with a chuckle. "I knew you had an eye for him, Joa Marie."

I clasp my palm over my forehead and rest my elbow on my desk.

Do truly I care right now or is this nothing more than innocent curiosity?

"Hey, Mom, thanks for getting back to me. I've got a few things to take care of, so I'll let you go," I say, holding my breath as I wait for her response.

"Sounds good, sweetheart. Talk to you later." Mom hangs up.

She's never been a woman of few words.

Either they had a secret heart-to-heart about me, or she's actually respecting my wishes and letting this go.

A knock on my door pulls my attention away, and when I glance up, I find Reed York himself showing himself in and closing the door behind him. Guess he couldn't be bothered to wait for me to say, "Come in."

"Can I help you?" I ask, sitting back in my chair and crossing my legs tight.

The New York email is displayed across my screen, but I don't bother hiding it. I haven't decided what I'm going to do yet, and even if I decide to go, it's not like that choice would have anything to do with him.

Reed runs a hand through his sandy hair, pacing slightly before staring past me and out to the wintry city beyond my window.

"What are you doing? Why are you acting so weird?" I ask.

He bites his lip before his diamond eyes snap to mine. "I can't stop thinking about what you said yesterday."

"I said a lot of things yesterday. Can you be more specific?"

Reed swallows, resting his hands on his angled hips. "When you said there was a time you thought you could see yourself dating me."

I laugh. "Out of everything I said yesterday, that's the one thing you can't stop thinking about?"

He nods.

"Is that why you were so quiet on the ride in?"

"Part of it. Yeah," he says, studying me. "Is it true, what you said?"

"Does it matter?"

"Of course it does. I wouldn't be standing here, willing to make an ass of myself if it didn't."

"You make an ass of yourself every day." I roll my eyes. "How is this any different?"

"Touché."

"Seriously, though, just let it go."

He comes around my desk.

"What are you doing?" I ask, looking him up and down.

"Just tell me, Joa. Yes or no. Did you mean what you said?"

I wait a beat, then another before finally answering.

"Yes," I say. "I meant it."

I watch as relief pours over his expression in real time.

"You liked me," he says, his lips cocked into a tentative smirk.

I push a breath through pursed lips. "Don't go getting a big head about it. Not like it means anything now, anyway."

"That's where you're wrong, Joa," he says. "It means *everything*."

I'm two seconds from laughing in his face and popping his hope-filled balloon when suddenly he takes my hands in his and pulls me to standing.

"Joa." My name is soft on his cinnamon breath, and my heart beats so hard in my ears that I can't think straight.

Reed's fingers find my hair and before I realize it, my mouth aligns with his.

I'd be lying if I said I hadn't thought about that kiss we shared in my room dozens of times in the past twenty-four hours.

But it was reckless of me to allow that to happen.

And foolish of me to secretly want it.

"My life hasn't been the same without you," he says, his voice like a whisper. "I miss you. I miss us."

"There never was an us, Reed," I say. "You're idealizing."

"There was always an us, Joa, and you know it."

Before I can protest, his mouth crushes mine and he lifts me up onto my desk. I crane my neck to ensure the blinds and closed—they are, thank God—before my lips return to his.

I want to stop.

I know I should stop.

But I can't.

I'm powerless at his touch.

He pushes my skirt up my sides before reaching up and sliding my silk panties down my thighs. His lips press into my neck, his cologne filling my lungs. My fingertips graze the side of his cheek before slipping to the nape of his neck, and I brace myself with my other hand as he pushes his body against mine with an animalistic fervor.

His slacks are unzipped and the outline of his rock-hard cock bulges through his boxers, and the sensation of wet heat invades the space between my legs, where his fingertips work my slit and his thumb circles my clit.

He was always so gentle, so steady, so intentional in the way he touched me—like he actually cared about my pleasure.

"There hasn't been anyone since you," he whispers into my ear before our gazes lock. He doesn't say it, but he's hoping I'll say the same.

And I do.

Because it's true.

"I haven't been with anyone else either," I say between kisses. It's a truth that both confuses and upsets me.

I tried to move on.

I tried blind dates and dating apps and after-hours network functions. I put myself out there. I made the connections.

None of them had half the chemistry I had with Reed.

I hated him for it.

But mostly, I hated myself for comparing all of them to the one man who broke my heart into a billion pieces without so much as an inkling that it was coming.

I should've been looking for the antidote to Reed York.

Instead, I found myself looking for a replacement. Or at least someone to give me a fix.

But none of them kissed like him.

None of them pushed my buttons the way he did.

None of them looked at me the way he always did, like he was two seconds from devouring me, like I was the most magnificent thing in the world.

He kisses my neck and I exhale, widening my thighs as he lowers himself onto me. I gasp when he enters me, and I feel it in every part of my body.

My skin is on fire, my lungs empty.

He tastes my mouth as he fucks me, his thrusts alternating between greedy and needy and slow and steady. He can't decide if he wants all of me right this instant or if he wants to savor this moment.

Deep down, I think we both know this is it.

A farewell fuck, as unpoetic as that may seem.

Hate sex.

Though I'm pretty sure the hate part is extremely one-sided.

Reed drives himself into me, deeper, harder, and I hold on tight, my knees braced against his sides. It isn't until later that I realize there's a stapler jammed against my back. We used to be pros at this office sex thing. This is just sloppy.

The flutter in my middle and the building intensity between my legs signals I'm getting close. I squeeze the back of his arm and kiss him harder—it was always my tell, and his thrusts grow quicker.

We come at the same time, just like old times.

The release is epic.

The aftershocks of the orgasmic wave radiate through every part of me.

But when we're finished, we're just a couple of broken,

breathless souls in wrinkled office wear with nothing to say as we put ourselves back together.

Our eyes hold in the moment before he leaves.

I wait for him to speak, but all he gives me is silence and a stare that I can't possibly read.

I'm not sure who I hate more: him for hurting me a year ago and weaseling his way back into my life? Or me for letting it happen after I promised myself it wouldn't.

PAST

Joa

My office looks like a war zone by the time we're finished. Papers everywhere. Pens littering the floor. Chair shoved against the door so the cleaning crew wouldn't accidentally barge in.

I'm trying to piece my dress back together, turning it right-side in, but the attached slip is caught on something.

Reed is perched on the edge of my desk, a few feet from me, the lucky bastard is already fully clothed. I'm sure he's enjoying the view right now—me struggling in nothing but a demi-lace bra and matching thong.

The smell of arousal lingers in the air, mixing with his Creed cologne.

My body misses his body already.

"How much longer are you going to stare?" I ask when I finally fix my dress situation.

He reaches for me, wrapping his hand around my wrist and pulling me against him. His hands slide down the small of my back before making a detour at my ass and giving it a hard squeeze.

"You have no idea how sexy you are, do you?" he asks.

I don't think I'm much different from most other women. When I look in the mirror, there are parts I don't mind and parts that have always bothered me, though they bother me less the older I get. But I've never once looked at myself and wallowed in my sexiness with unabashed confidence.

But he makes me feel sexy, the way he worships my body with his hands, the way he tastes every tender spot with his tongue ... unafraid to explore every inch like he owns it all.

I suppose in a way, he does.

18

REED

"ARE YOU GOING TO TAKE IT?" Lucy Clarke's voice drifts into the hall.

I'm passing Joa's office Friday afternoon. I need some fresh air. A breather. Next week is going to be brutal on everyone, and my mind is heavy.

I heard back from Scott with the Securities and Exchange Commission.

It's happening.

And I'd give anything to warn these people, but when a government official tells you to keep your mouth shut under any and all circumstances, you keep your damn mouth shut.

Glancing in, I spot Lucy sitting in Joa's guest chair, leaning forward and reading an email as Joa careens the computer monitor toward her.

"I think I will," I hear Joa say. "New York could be fun, you know? And it's not all that different from Chicago."

Wait. She applied for a position in New York?

I knock on the door, interrupting their little chat. "Running out to grab some coffee. Anyone want anything?"

"I'd love one. Mocha frappe for me please, skinny, no whip," Lucy says.

Joa's eyes are smiling. This New York offer apparently has her in good spirits.

Lucy's curious stare passes between us before she pops out of her seat. "I'll be in my office if anyone needs me ..."

"You're moving to New York?" I ask.

"You were eavesdropping?" The smile fades from her baby blues.

"Your door was open. I was passing by. Happened to hear," I say. "Regardless ... you're leaving Chicago? I thought you loved Chicago."

She shrugs. "I do love Chicago. And it'll always be home. And I can always come back. I'm just getting that itch again, the urge to spread my wings a bit. I haven't been on vacation since ..."

She doesn't finish her thought. She doesn't have to.

"Anyway, Ian offered me a position out there," she says. "And I'm taking it."

"Ian?" I ask. "Iaconelli? From the Manhattan branch?"

"Yes. That Ian."

I thought she was taking some random job out there—I didn't realize it was an internal transfer.

"My lease is due for a renewal at the end of the month anyway, so the timing is perfect," she says. "And I've already spoken to Harold. He says if I'm not feeling it, I'll always have a place back here."

"Don't take it."

She laughs. "What?"

"Don't take it."

"Yeah. I heard you. I just ... what is this? What are you

doing?" Her eyes squint and she rises from her chair, arms folding. "Do you think this is about you?"

"No, I—"

"—you do. Why else would you care? Why else would you want to stop me?" she asks.

"Just ... you have to trust me."

"That's the funniest thing I think you've ever said, Reed," she says, shutting down her computer.

"It's only three. Where are you going?"

"Home. Calling it a day. Should probably start packing. They want me there after the first of the year."

I'd give anything to tell her sooner, but my hands are tied. Leaking this information would be a federal violation with severe consequences. People would start dumping GenCoins left and right and then the finance industry would know ahead of the announcement, which would be disastrous.

She grabs her purse from a drawer in her desk, slinging it over her shoulder.

"You're the most infuriating human I've ever known, Reed York," she says. "And you have a lot of nerve."

And then she's gone.

PAST

Reed

I tip the bartender and ask him to change the TV to the Bloomberg channel.

"This is insane." Joa runs her fingers through her hair, her eyes wild and lit. "It doesn't seem real. How is this real?"

She laughs with watery eyes, one hand curved around a French 75.

Today, the value of GenCoins more than doubled—a historic first in cryptocurrency. And on top of that, we received an endorsement from Paul Fieldstone, one of the richest billionaires in the world, a self-taught investor with his ear to the ground.

The first time Paul Tweeted about GenCoin was shortly after eight o'clock this morning.

Prices soared.

The second time he Tweeted was around three in the afternoon.

That's when we officially doubled.

We must have thousands of seven-digit portfolios across our three branches and now? A significant portion of them are officially eight-digit portfolios.

I toss back a mouthful of bourbon, eyes glued to the screen. These astronomical hikes in prices can make a man feel like a million bucks, but the higher they climb, the harder they can fall. With cryptos being so new, they're still a bit volatile and unpredictable, but anything can happen.

Analysts have been saying for years, there's an eighty percent chance GenCoins will surpass a quarter of a million dollars apiece in the next two decades.

Only time will tell.

She hasn't stopped grinning since we left the office over an hour ago. Joa looks on the outside the way I feel on the inside.

Warm. Grateful. Beside herself with excitement.

But it isn't the rush of the money that's getting to me.

For the first time in my life, I'm celebrating something with someone who shares my enthusiasm. Someone who gets me. Someone who can't stop flinging her arms around my shoulders, trying to simultaneously bounce on her toes and kiss me at the same time.

There isn't another feeling in the world like it.

I hope it never goes away.

19

Joa

MY BODY TREMBLES and shudders the whole train ride home, but I'm not cold.

I'm furious.

Outside the window, the world is in a Christmas hangover. It's always been a strange and jarring sight to see Christmas decorations the day after, to hear some of the stations and shops still playing holiday music.

It's almost as if we know we don't need it, but we're also not quite ready to let it go.

So we're stuck in that gray period—the week before Christmas and New Year's when we're exhausted from one celebration and biding our time before we move on to the next in the meantime.

It almost feels like a metaphor for my life right now. I'm in a low valley, stuck between two peaks. Only my next peak will be here before I know it.

Once upon a time, I might have dared to say Reed York was a peak in my life.

I called Ian on my walk to the station and accepted the position. It was the strangest thing, though …

I didn't feel better afterwards.

I thought I might feel free or vindicated in some little way, but instead, I felt this heaviness in the pit of my stomach, almost a gut instinct questioning whether or not I made the right choice.

Digging my phone from my bag, I send a text to Lucy, asking if she wants to meet up for drinks this weekend to celebrate my transfer.

Another text comes through from a group text I'm a part of—a bunch of girls from high school are back in Mills Haven for the holidays, and they want to meet up.

Between Lucy and my old friends and the early stages of packing and searching for a last-minute place in New York, I should have no problem keeping my mind off Reed this weekend.

PAST

Joa

Warm sunlight filters in through the Cabo San Lucas casita windows as we listen to the waves crash against the cliffs.

His fingers trace my bare skin, exploring the peaks and valleys of my body as if it's the first time he's ever really seen me.

For months we've been doing this, and I keep waiting for the day he decides he's grown bored with me—or vice versa.

But the more time I spend with him, the more I find myself quietly looking forward to the next time. I've even stooped so low as to steal a few things off his desk here and there when he's not paying attention, just so I had an excuse to return them.

His palm glides down my caved stomach, stopping just between my partially spread thighs where he takes his time circling my clit with his thumb.

I'm still sensitive from the last orgasm, but still, I pulse to life the moment he slips a finger inside me.

Someone once said that life can be reduced to a series of peaks and valleys when you look at the big picture.

Reed York?

He's a peak.

No question.

20

REED

THERE'S a knock at my door just before eleven Saturday morning. I can't remember the last time I slept in this late—but a weighted blanket of exhaustion clings to me anyway.

I throw on a pair of sweats and a t-shirt and head out of the master bedroom.

"Delivery for Mr. York," a deepened, muffled voice says.

Glancing through the peephole, I find a familiar blonde in a faux-fur stole standing on the other side.

Her balled fist lifts to knock again, but I pull the door open.

"Bijou, what are you doing here?" I ask.

"Surprise!" She flings her arms around my shoulders.

"When you asked for the address, you said you were sending a gift."

"Oh, come on," she says, swatting at me as she wheels her Louis Vuitton suitcase inside my rented apartment.

"You hate opening presents and I hate shopping for other people. You can't tell me you didn't see this coming."

She deposits her suitcase in the middle of the living room.

"This place is kind of small for you, don't you think?" she asks.

"It's fine. I won't be here much longer."

"Where's the guest room?" She rises on her toes, careening her neck toward the hall.

"It's a one-bedroom."

"Ew." She sticks out her tongue.

Like I said ... cut from two extremely different cloths. Sewn together by two entirely different tailors. Only thing we have in common is our DNA.

I blame my parents for spoiling her though.

My mother always dreamed of having a little girl someday, but after she delivered me, there were some complications. Doctors told her she'd never be able to get pregnant again ... then four years later, along came little Bijou.

Their little trinket.

The jewel of my parents' eyes.

I don't resent Bijou for the way she is. It isn't her fault. Redford and Bebe created this mess. It doesn't make her any less my sister, and she's the only sibling I have.

My sister takes a seat on the microfiber sofa that anchors the small living room and then she takes a look around, her manicured brows lifting into her smooth forehead.

"You're bored already," I tell her. "You should've stayed back in LA. Trust me, all I do here is work. I won't have time to entertain you."

Her jaw falls. "Reed Redford Bennington York, you do not need to entertain me. I'm not a child."

"All right." I head to the kitchen and grab a beer from the fridge, pointing it at her. "I'm holding you to that."

"We should FaceTime Mom and Dad," she says, holding her phone in front of her face and fussing with her hair as she uses the reverse camera as a mirror. "They're probably worried about me. We should let them know I made it."

The sad thing is, she isn't wrong.

They worry about her constantly. Me? I once went to Yemen on a business trip and they didn't even break a sweat. In fact, they forgot I'd even left LA.

I uncap my bottle and toss a few sips back. "Sure."

She taps her screen a couple of times and sinks back into the sofa, drawing her legs in.

"Hi, Mom! Hi, Dad!" she says. "You guys look nice and tan. Did you have a good time?"

"Hi, Angel." My father speaks first.

"Darling, I take it you've made it safely to Chicago? Where's your brother? Is he with you?" my mother asks.

Bijou waves me over. "Yeah. He's just standing here drinking a beer and trying not to act like he's annoyed that I'm here."

I shoot her a look.

It couldn't be further from the truth.

It's just … not a good time, and for reasons I can't get into with her.

"Reed, is that true?" my mother asks.

I take a seat beside my sister and make an appearance on our end of the call.

"Not at all." I force a smile and hook my arm around my sister's shoulders, messing up her hair in the process. "It's a nice surprise. She's just mad she's going to have to sleep on the pull-out sofa."

"Oh, dear." My mother gasps. "Bij, would you like your father to book you a room at the Four Seasons?"

"You guys, it's fine. I came here to see Reed, so I'm just going to stay here. And if my neck hurts in the morning, I'll just get a massage somewhere," she says. "Anyway, I'm starving, so I'm going to make Reed order some pizza or something." She nudges me. "Good pizza, not chain pizza."

"All right, darlings," my mother says. "You two enjoy your time together. We'll see you when you get back."

"Bye-bye now," my father says, lifting a crystal tumbler filled with amber-colored liquor.

Bijou presses the red button on the screen and lets her phone fall in her lap with a light thud.

"I'm seriously starving," she says. "Are there any good pizza places around here? Isn't Chicago known for its pizza or something?"

"You're thinking of Chicago-style pizza," I say. "It's like deep-dish."

I don't mention the calories to her or I'll never hear the end of it.

"There are some menus on the side of the fridge. Help yourself. I'm going to hit the shower." I get off the couch and trek down the hall. I'll do just about anything for my sister, but I won't be her little bitch. She's perfectly capable of ordering pizza herself.

"Ugh. Rude," she says, though I know she's teasing. Deep down, I think she appreciates the fact that I'm the one person who doesn't enable her spoiled-princess-ness.

A few minutes later, I'm standing under a spray of hot water, unmoving and contemplating the day's plans now that my sister has thrown a bit of a wrench in them.

Originally I thought about trying to get a hold of Joa,

trying to talk to her a little more about the New York position without giving anything away—if that's even possible

The SEC wants me to wait until January 2nd to make
the announcement.

This means six more days of Joa hating me.

Six more days of office tension so ripe it's begging to be
plucked.

Fucking her on her desk yesterday, as incredible as it
was, wasn't planned. It just happened. I went into her office
with the simple intention of confronting her about what she
said so I could finally get an answer and stop ruminating ...
and then I kissed her.

And once I started, I couldn't stop.

When she kissed me back, I was too far gone.

It was happening and there was no stopping it, though I
don't think either of us would've stopped it regardless.

When it was over, we straightened ourselves up,
exchanged a look, and I left.

I wasn't sure what to say, and she was looking at me
with this bewildered glint in her eyes as she tugged and
straightened her skirt, and leaving just seemed like the right
thing to do in that moment.

I figured we'd talk about it later, when we'd both caught
our breaths and composed ourselves.

And then the New York thing happened.

Letting the hot water drip down me in thick rivulets, I
reach for a bottle of shampoo and work up a lather. It smells
like Joa, and that makes me just as happy as it makes me sad.

Maybe space is good this weekend.

We can start fresh on Monday.

PAST

Reed

"Who are you texting?" Bijou stands on the other side of my kitchen island, scrutinizing my every move apparently.

"A friend from work."

"Girl or guy?"

"Woman. Why?"

She smacks the quartz counter. "I knew it!"

"And what is it you think you know?" I slip my phone back into my pocket. As dense and self-centered as my sister can be sometimes, she can be eerily perceptive.

"You like her," Bijou says. "Your face lights every time your phone dings. You're like one of those dogs with the bells."

"Pavlov's dogs."

"Yeah. That. Anyway, you had this stupid-looking little half-grin on your face when you were texting her just a second ago. You wouldn't make that face if you didn't like her."

"I don't like her—not like that," I lie. "But I do like to spend time with her. And spending time with her makes me smile. It doesn't mean that I like her."

She waves a hand and rolls her eyes. "And now you're just talking in circles and making negative sense while you're at it."

"Isn't there a sale at Barney's going on?"

Bijou slides off the bar stool. "I can take a hint, Reedster. I'll leave, but not because there's a sale at Barney's and not because you're uncomfortable talking about this girl that you allegedly don't like, but because I want to. And I have a wax at four and traffic's a bitch this time of day."

I walk my sister to the door, where she steps into her crystal-studded Louboutins and turns to face me.

"Look, I don't know who this girl is and I don't care if you like her or if you don't like her," she says. "But as a woman who's tired of men saying one thing and doing another, whatever you do, just be honest with yourself. And with her. No games. K? Bye."

I shut the door behind her just as another text from Joa buzzes in my pocket.

Before I get a chance to read it, I catch a glimpse of my reflection in the mirror above the entry console.

Goddamn it.

Bijou was right.

21

Joa

THIS MUST BE what dying feels like.

I flush the toilet Monday morning and gather a wad of toilet paper to dab at my mouth. I swear my body's going to be in a permanent C-shape after this.

My back throbs when I shuffle toward the sink. Sleeping on a bathroom floor will do that. And I rinse my mouth out with cold tap water before swishing with spearmint mouthwash that nearly makes me gag.

"I never get sick, my ass," I mumble to myself, recalling my routine doctor's visit back in November when I bragged about not having been sick for three straight winters.

My stomach churns, alternating between feeling empty and hungry and nauseous and sometimes all three at once, and I brace myself on the counter before grabbing a thermometer.

103.4.

My stomach squeezes and a dry heave follows.

Guess I'm staying home today.

Heading back to my room, I darken the blinds, climb under the covers, grab my phone off the nightstand, and text Harold to let him know I'm not going to be in today. As soon as I hear back from him, I shut my phone off and go back to sleep.

PAST

Joa

I pass Reed's office door a quarter after ten, only to find his lights are off and the handle is locked.

That's odd.

Then again, it was unusually quiet around here this morning.

I head back, stopping at the front desk to ask Lena if she knows where he is.

"Called in sick," she says, cradling her phone's receiver on her shoulder. "Poor thing sounded horrible. Could hardly tell it was him."

As soon as I get back to my desk, I pull out my phone and Door Dash him some chicken soup from his favorite deli on Sunset along with a note that reads: **This doesn't mean anything other than get well soon so you can get your Malibu Ken-looking ass back to the office**.

We're friends now.
I think.
And this is the kind of thing friends do for each other.

22

REED

"YES, Joa, I'll let everyone know." Pam hangs up her phone as I pass her desk Tuesday morning.

"Joa's sick again today?" I ask.

She glances across the top of her desk. "Yes. Poor thing. Fever still won't break. She sounds awful, too."

I'd be lying if I said a part of me isn't suspicious. Pam could be covering for her and she might be biding her time until I leave.

She was out Monday, she's out today, and if she's out tomorrow and we're closed Thursday for New Year's Day, that means she'll only have to see me one more day before I go.

I work from the conference room for two hours that morning before deciding to take a bit of a field trip to Mills Haven. With my laptop in tow, I let Pam know I'll be telecommuting the rest of the day, and I make a quick stop before ordering an Uber.

HOLY SHIT.

She looks like death warmed over.

First of all, I'm surprised that she answered the door.

Second of all, I feel a little bad for doubting her sickness. She's clearly going through some shit.

Greasy hair is piled in a messy bun on top of her head, and her skin is the color of the driven snow that surrounds her brownstone. From what I can tell, she appears to have on two layers of pajamas plus a robe, all of it hanging loosely off her frame.

"What are you doing here?" she asks, voice scratchy.

I lift the brown bag in my hand. "Brought you soup."

Her eyes go in and out of focus and she stands in the doorway for what feels like forever. I get the sense that she wants to say something clever, but she doesn't have the strength, physical, mental, or otherwise.

"You can come in," she says, though it's more of a defeated mumble than anything else.

I follow her, latching the door behind me. The place feels like night, every shade drawn, every blind darkened.

The TV in the living room is muted and paused on an episode of Real Housewives of Beverly Hills, and a messy pile of blankets rests on the floor next to the couch.

Tissues and empty glasses of orange juice litter the coffee table, and I can't help but wonder if she's always been a bit of a slob or if this is purely the sickness taking its toll.

Her office was always so tidy, and she was always so particular about putting things back exactly the way they were. I'm choosing to believe the latter.

Joa collapses on the sofa, her hand slapped across her forehead as her eyes wince.

"I'm sure you're starving. Can you hold anything down?" I ask, taking the cushion next to her feet.

"Yeah," she says, half pointing to an open package of saltines on the side table.

"Good." I take the soup from its Styrofoam container and remove the lid. Steam escapes from the top as I place it on the coffee table and position it in front of her. "Eat, Joa. Even if you don't feel like it."

"Why are you here?" she asks as I help her sit up. Reaching for the plastic spoon I've laid out, she turns to me. "You thought I was faking it, didn't you?"

I smirk.

"Bastard." She ladles chicken broth into her plastic cutlery and lifts it to her full lips. "Not everything I do is because of you."

"I know that."

She presses play on her remote and she doesn't ask me to leave. Fifteen minutes later, she's managed to finish a third of her soup, and I refrigerate the rest of it.

"When was the last time you took something?" I ask, eyeing the vast collection of cold and flu meds accumulating on her kitchen counter.

"I don't know ... last night I think?"

I pop a couple of tablets from a tin packet and pour her a fresh glass of orange juice.

Look at me—taking care of someone.

If my friends could see me now ...

This trip has been chock full of all kinds of firsts.

Returning to the sofa, I hand over the pills and juice and help her get situated back under the covers. A moment later, she closes her eyes and she's out cold.

With her legs sprawled over my lap, I'm more or less pinned, and if I move too much I'm going to wake her, so I slowly reach for the remote and find something to watch to keep myself occupied until she wakes up or needs something again.

I tune her TV to ESPN and keep the volume as low as I can. Every few minutes, I steal a peak at this Snow White incarnate with her onyx hair, fair skin, and ruby lips. She'd look so peaceful if she wasn't shivering.

Her eyes flutter open and she rolls to her side, tugging the covers up around her neck.

"It's so cold in here. Can you turn up the heat?" she asks, her voice muffled by the blankets.

I slide out from beneath her legs and locate her thermostat, which is already set at 78. I bump it up to 80 and yank my sweater off, leaving my undershirt in place.

When I return to the sofa, I place my palm across her forehead and then her cheeks.

She's on fire.

"I'm freezing," she says through chattering teeth. "Can't get warm."

"The meds should kick in soon." I watch her lying there, helpless, and it damn near kills me. "Here ..."

I take my seat and then I take her hands, pulling her against me. Her skin burns to the touch, but she still shivers, even under five blankets. I'm hopeful my body heat might help a bit.

It's better than nothing.

And it's a hell of a lot better than sitting here watching her suffer.

A few minutes pass when I finally realize she's stopped shaking. Her eyes are closed, but I don't think she's quite asleep yet.

I take the opportunity to watch her, to study her features the way I used to ... before. The bend of her brows.

The cupid's bow of her upper lip. The fan of dark lashes splaying out from her hooded eyelids.

"Reed?" she says my name so soft, I almost think I'm hearing things.

"Yes?"

"Why couldn't you have just said no?"

Her body melts against mine before I have a chance to reply, and her breathing steadies. She's out now. And it's for the best.

She needs her rest.

And I need more time.

In three days, I'll be able to tell her everything.

PAST

Reed

"Ow." Joa picks at the pad of her left ring finger, her knees drawn up to her chest as she sits in a lounge chair off a breezy Aruban patio.

The sea breeze tousles a strand of dark hair across her forehead, but she leaves it. She's too focused on whatever's going on with her finger.

"What's wrong?" I ask, leaning against the frame of the sliding glass door, a coffee in my hand.

"Splinter." She frowns.

"Let me see it." I reach for her hand, but she jerks it away.

"I've got it."

She's a stubborn little thing sometimes. I guess it's okay for her to Door Dash soup to my apartment when I'm out sick, but God forbid I try to help her with a splinter.

"Clearly you don't," I say.

The pad of her finger is growing red and irritated, and the fact that I can see it from where I'm standing tells me it's a big one.

I take the chair beside her and scoot it closer. "You're making it worse."

Her shoulders fall and she blows a breath that moves the errant strand of hair out of her eyes. She knows I'm right.

"Here."

She offers her hand to me, and I turn it palm-side up, examining the wooden sliver lodged beneath her skin.

"It's deeper than it was a second ago," I say, trying to determine which end is the entrance point. Lifting her finger to my lips, I circle my tongue around the swollen skin until I feel the tip of the splinter.

She says nothing, simply watches me work, and a second later, it's out.

"That was fast," she says, checking it out when I'm done. "It's weird having someone tend to me like that who isn't my mom."

It's weird for me too. Nurture isn't something that's ever come easy to me. Growing up, if I was sick, my mother would have the nanny run me to the doctor or the ER. She thought hospital waiting rooms were the epitome of disgusting, and of course she always had some trip coming up, so possibly contracting an illness before was a risk she wasn't willing to take.

So the nanny would take me.

The nanny would answer the doctor's questions.

The nanny would relay everything to my parents.

There was never anyone to hold my hand during shots, never the soothing balm of a mother's voice telling me everything was going to be okay or that it would only hurt for a second.

"You can be pretty sweet when you want to be, York." She sweeps her hair over her shoulder and wears a smile just for me.

"Don't get used to it."

"Didn't plan on it."

23

Joa

I WAKE with a dry mouth and drenched hair that clings to my neck and forehead, buried under a mountain of covers that I fling off my body with as much strength as I can muster.

Sitting up, a rush of pain floods my head and neck.

That's what I get for sleeping on the couch ... how many nights now?

I don't know what day it is or how long I've been sleeping.

My pajamas cling to me and my itchy skin is covered in dampness. Without hesitating, I begin tearing them off, layer by layer, tossing them aside and basking in the rush of tepid hair that hits my flesh.

For a moment, I begin to see stars.

Maybe I stood up too fast?

And then ... everything goes black.

When I wake, I'm sitting in my bathtub—covered in

bubbles. The water is lukewarm but it's quite comfortable. I reach to my forehead, sliding off a cool washcloth I didn't realize was there.

I'm so confused.

Until I glance across the bathroom and find Reed leaning against the counter, aimlessly thumbing through his phone.

"Ah, there you are," he says, looking up.

"You did this?" I ask, sitting up. Bubbles gather around my breasts.

"You were burning up. And you passed out. As soon as you're cooled off, we should probably get you to drink something. I've called out for some Gatorade." He slips his phone back into his pocket. "I talked to one of my friends back home. He's a physician. He said you should be fine once we get you rehydrated since your fever's starting to break."

"You took my temperature?" I'd laugh at the image if I wasn't so exhausted.

He nods.

"What day is it?" I ask.

"Wednesday," he says. "And it's seven o'clock. At night."

"When did you get here?"

"Yesterday, just before noon. I brought you soup, remember?"

I squeeze my eyes and inhale the scent of lavender bubbles, trying to think back to yesterday. I vaguely remember someone ringing the doorbell. At least I think I remember. It all feels like a dream at this point.

"I let you in?" I ask with a slight chuckle.

"I know. Crazy, right?"

"What's with the bubbles." I lift a handful of them.

"Modesty."

He's thrown me another one of his curveballs, and I'm rendered speechless.

I sink back against the tub until the nape of my neck hits the top of the water, and I stare at the popcorn ceiling above the shower.

He's making it nearly impossible to hate him, despite the fact that forgiving him still feels out of the question.

I'm not there yet.

It's been a year, and I've yet to fully comprehend just why he did what he did and why he did it the way he did it.

I'm just supposed to accept that "he had no choice?" I'm just supposed to believe that and be okay with it? How is that fair to me? And what kind of message would that be sending to him? That he can go behind my back and hurt me and I'll give him chances every time?

I'm not that kind of woman.

I feel his eyes on me, and when I turn my attention in his direction, I find him lost in thought.

"It's too bad," I say.

"What's too bad?"

"That things didn't work out for us. That things happened the way they did. We might've had something pretty amazing, Reed."

His arms fold across his muscled chest. "It's not too late. I'm still there. I didn't go anywhere. You're the one who left, remember?"

"Right. And your actions are the reason I left, remember?"

"How could I forget? You remind me of it every chance you get."

"Can you blame me?" I ask, sitting up and drawing my knees against my chest. It feels odd arguing with him, reclined in a tub full of bubbles.

"No, Joa. I can't. And I've told you that. I'm sorry." His full lips flatten and his arms tighten. His stare weighs me down and we linger in silence, shooting looks and holding our tongues.

How many times has he apologized and not once has he said anything about wishing he hadn't done it at all, wishing he could take it back, wishing he would've done it differently?

Not once.

If you hurt someone you care about and you don't regret it, are you truly sorry?

His phone buzzes in his pocket and he checks the screen. "I have to take this."

He leaves me alone with my thoughts in a tub of tepid water. Chills begin to run through me and sweat collects across my brow.

I think I'm going to be sick again.

PAST

Joa

My naked body slides against his, a rush of warm water passing between us, beside us, and all around us.

This weekend has marked a handful of firsts for me.

First time having sex in a bathtub.

First time in Seattle.

First time catching Reed looking at me like he's hiding secret thoughts behind his glinting irises.

I don't bother asking him what he's thinking about. He wouldn't tell me if I begged. He's the epitome of a closed book when it comes to anything deeper than his perfected exterior.

"I think there's more water on the floor than there is in the tub." I sit up and move to the opposite side of the behemoth Jacuzzi in the condo we're renting, waiting until I catch my breath. "We should clean up. I hope we have enough towels ..."

He hasn't moved. He's still resting his back against his

end of the tub, one muscled arm behind his head as he watches me.

Bracing myself, I rise so I can climb out and mop up the wet floor, only before I so much as hike a leg over the ledge, Reed's hand hooks around my left thigh.

"What are you doing?" I chuckle. He can't possibly be ready for another round.

Saying nothing, he pulls me back into the warm water, guiding me onto him and slipping my arms around his shoulders.

My body slides against his, weightless almost, and I can't help but notice he isn't hard. This isn't him trying to get laid again.

"What is this?" I ask, resting my chin on his chest and staring up at him.

"Just lay with me for a little bit," he says.

I lift a brow.

"Don't read into it, Jolivet. It just feels really good—relaxing, I mean." He's quick to clarify.

I don't disagree, so I press my cheek against his chest and listen to his heart as warm water gently laps around us.

We stay here, like this, until the water cools.

24

REED

I TAKE my phone call with the SEC outside, on Joa's front porch, watching my breath turn to clouds that quickly evaporate into a darkening gray sky.

I try to keep it as brief as I can, knowing she's still in the bath and will need help getting out, but by the time the call ends, the screen tells me it's been thirteen minutes and four seconds.

A car pulls up just before I go in, and a scrawny kid in a military-style parka runs a bag of Gatorade to me. I sign the receipt, slip him a tip, and head in.

When I return to the bathroom, the tub is drained and Joa's nowhere to be found.

I find her a minute later, lying on the sofa, dressed in a t-shirt and plaid cotton shorts, a blanket half covering her lap.

She's almost asleep, but she's due for her medicine.

"Joa," I say, veering into the kitchen and popping a couple of pills from a tin packet. "Don't fall asleep yet."

I pour some blue Gatorade into a cup and bring everything to her. She swallows them with two small gulps and lies back down. I thought she was on the mend, hoped maybe we were making progress, but now I'm not so sure.

"Drink a little more before you go back to sleep," I say, thinking back to what my doctor friend had told me on the phone earlier.

"*Fluids, fluids, fluids, and more fluids*," he'd said.

She sits up a little, taking tiny sips from her cup, her eyes glassy and unfocused on the muted TV.

"It's New Year's Eve," she says.

"It is."

She's quiet for a moment, like she wants to ask if I'm staying or leaving, but she can't bring herself to.

I adjust the volume on the TV when I can't stand the tension anymore, and she settles back into the sofa cushions, wrapping her blanket around her body.

It doesn't take long for her to drift to sleep again, and I head to her kitchen table to crack my laptop and get some more work done, but before I get started, I shoot a text to her mother with an update.

Bevin had asked if she should come over, offering to relieve me, but I told her I had it and I'd keep her in the loop if anything changed. I get the feeling that backing off and letting someone else take care of her baby isn't normally her cup of tea, but she didn't protest. I did, however, ask if she could drop off some clothes for me since I didn't want to run back to the city. Within twenty minutes, she'd sent Tom over with a grocery sack full of some of Logan's old jeans and t-shirts, all of which appeared to be circa 2007 when he was clearly going through some kind of Ed Hardy phase.

Why Bevin still has this stuff, I don't know. I'm just grateful it fits.

The screen of my phone lights as I pull up my email, and Bijou's name fills the screen. A quick glance toward the living room tells me Joa's out again.

"Hey," I answer, keeping my voice down. "What's up?"

"Are you ever coming back to this ... *quaint* ... little apartment you rented?"

"I'm sorry. Some things came up." I delete a couple of junk emails and read a memo from IT—not that it's going to be relevant after this week. "You doing okay?"

She blows a breath into the phone. "Yeah, just bored. It's too cold to do anything fun."

"You knew I was here for work, Bij."

"Whatever. Are you coming back to the city tonight or not? One of my friends from USC is actually here this week and she invited us to a party at the Godfrey. You in?"

I look to Joa again, who appears to be halfway between dead and sleeping.

"Probably not."

My sister is silent on the other end. She's always been more of a pouter than a yeller, and I can picture her sulking right now, sitting in the middle of a shit-brown microfiber sofa in a modest one-bedroom apartment.

Can't help but chuckle at the image I've conjured in my head.

"Have fun tonight, Bij," I say. "And be safe."

"You're lame." She hangs up and I return to my emails, though I appear to be all caught up. With the holidays, everyone's either checked off the schedule or checked out completely.

Now, we wait.

I return to the sofa, lifting Joa's feet, placing them in my lap and covering them with her blanket. Flipping through the channels, I settle on some History Channel documentary and rest my eyes, letting the soothing voice of the narrator lull me to sleep.

When I wake, the TV is blasting with an air fryer informercial, bright and loud, and I scramble for the remote and mute it before it wakes Joa.

The guide on the TV says it's 11:58.

Almost midnight.

Almost a new year.

I tune to one of the local channels where Ryan Seacrest is preparing to lead a countdown from Times Square and the camera pans to some pop band taking the stage.

The crowd is filled with people from all walks of life, but mostly they're the young, dumb, and broke type, the ones most likely to live in the moment and make decisions without thinking about the consequences.

Enjoy that freedom while it lasts, kids.

A timer fills the bottom of the screen; sixty seconds.

Fifty-nine ...

Fifty-eight ...

If Joa hadn't gotten sick, I wonder if we would've reconciled this week. I wonder if we'd be celebrating the new year together—between the sheets or otherwise.

I watch her sleep a little longer, her hand tucked under her cheek.

Ten.

Nine.

Eight.

Seven.

Six.

Five.

Four.

Three.

Two.

One.

The ball drops.

The screen fills with balloons and confetti, people cheering, people kissing.

I should go.

Today's Thursday. I make the big announcement tomorrow morning, and I fly home tomorrow afternoon. Lots to do between now and then. Lots to think about too.

Rising from the sofa, I adjust her blanket before depositing a kiss on her forehead.

"Happy New Year," I say, my voice low and soft. She doesn't stir.

I gather my things, trying not to make a sound, and before I go, I scribble a note and leave it on the counter, asking her to call me first thing Friday morning.

I want her to hear it from me first.

PAST

Reed

I look up from my desk to find Joa standing in my doorway in a navy pantsuit, nude heels, and pearls, her hair pulled away from her face.

Shit.

First round interviews for the VP position was today.

"Hey, how'd it go?" I ask, pretending I'm not silently fantasizing about ripping that entire stuffy outfit off that taut body.

She takes a seat across from me. "I think it went pretty well, actually."

"You going back home this week? For Thanksgiving?" I ask.

"I decided to stick around. I'm going home next month for Christmas, so I'll see everyone then. Neve said she could FaceTime me in to dinner, but one of my neighbors is having a friendsgiving thing, so I'll probably go to that for a little bit. What about you? Any plans?"

I turn my attention to a new batch of emails that fill my inbox. "I really hope this isn't you trying to invite me along to your weird friendsgiving thing."

"I'm offended that you would even suggest that." She swats at me. "You should know me better than that by now."

I delete an email before moving to the next. "Just making sure."

I pretend not to notice the way her expression fades, and she pretends she's got some work to catch up on.

We've been hooking up almost a year now, and we've managed not to break a single rule.

No hotels.

No couple selfies.

No visiting each other's places.

But holidays were never off-limits. Hell, Memorial Day Weekend was one for the books, but I draw the line at Thanksgiving and Christmas and the kinds of holidays that involve introducing the person you've been seeing to your family and kissing under mistletoe.

I hope I didn't hurt her feelings, but I just can't.

But New Year's? That's fair game.

There's no one else I'd rather kiss this year.

25

Joa

THE SUN PEEKS through my bedroom curtains, baking a warm spot into my pillow.

I don't know what day it is, what time it is, or when I migrated from the sofa to the bed, but one thing's for sure: my head doesn't hurt anymore.

Also, I can breathe through my nostrils again. Kind of.

And my stomach isn't churning.

I wouldn't say I'm one hundred percent, but I think I'm finally on the up and up.

Rubbing my eyes, I peer around the room for my phone before discovering it's lost somewhere between the sheets and the comforter.

The lockscreen tells me it's 11:01 am, Friday, January 2nd.

I basically Rip Van Winkle'd myself through this entire week.

Impressive.

I go to the window next, shielding my eyes as I adjust the curtains and blinds so it no longer feels like a permanent state of nighttime in my room.

It must have snowed again. My half of the driveway is covered in pure, undriven white fluff and giant snowflakes fall from the sky, seemingly in slow motion.

Shuffling to the bathroom, I brush the fuzz from my teeth and gargle away the taste of sickness from my mouth before running a shower.

Inhaling a lungful of hot, steamy air through my nose, I vow never to take breathing for granted again.

Running out to the kitchen to grab a quick drink of water to soothe my parched throat before I wash up for the day, I stop when I find a handwritten note on the peninsula.

JOA—

It was kind of nice hanging out with the version of you who couldn't talk back.

Hope you're feeling better.

Call me Friday morning.

—Reed

I PUSH his note aside as bits and pieces of the last few days begin to fill my memory, though it's very much like a puzzle with missing pieces.

Before I talk to him again, I need to answer some questions of my own.

Was he only being nice because he wanted something ... that something being me?

Was it genuine?

And does any of this change anything? Obviously, judging by the tone of his note he's acting like we're friends now.

But is that even possible?

Hitting the shower, I scrub myself until I smell like a fairy garden and shampoo my hair until it squeaks. Already I feel even better than I did ten minutes ago when I rolled out of bed.

As soon as I'm finished and I've had a chance to dry my hair and change into some clean sweats, I search for my phone so I can text Harold and let him know I'm planning to stay home one last day despite the fact that it's now almost noon and he probably already assumes that. But still, the communication studies part of me can't resist.

While I no longer feel like a catatonic zombie, I still think I should take a day to make sure it's all out of my system.

I locate my phone on my nightstand where I left it, and wake the screen only to discover that eleven text messages await me.

I tap on the green icon and scroll through the senders, reading their messages one by one:

LUCY: **omg, joa. turn on the news.**

DAD: **Just heard. You doing okay, kiddo?**

NEVE: **I can't believe it … I'm literally in shock right now.**

LOGAN: **Well shit. There goes my get rich quick plan.**

MOM: **Joa, sweetheart. We're worried sick. Call us or we'll be stopping by in an hour to check on you.**

REED: **Joa, call me. Please.**

I TOSS my phone on the bed and flip on the TV, tuning into a cable news channel where the first words I see scrolling across the bottom of the screen are:

GENCOIN IN TROUBLE. FUTURE OF CRYPTOCURRENCY IN QUESTION.

I'm dreaming.

This has to be a dream.

There's no way this is real.

The woman on the screen is using words like fraud and market manipulation and SEC investigation.

The screen cuts away to three side-by-side images: Elliot Grosvenor, Harold Coffey, and Ian Iaconelli. The next cutaway is a graph, where a red line illustrates the two-year price history of GenCoin and a caption reads: ***TODAY'S VALUE: $0. Down 100% from yesterday.***

"There you have it, folks," the host says. "GenCoin is a bust. We're going to bring in Professor Mitchell Greenley, finance department chair at Yale ..."

I collapse onto my bed.

How?

How could this have happened?

The last time I checked, which was less than a week ago, GenCoin was valued at over $21,000, up 500% from last year. We were bigger than Bitcoin, Litecoin, and Ethereum combined. The Wall Street Journal called us "unstoppable" and said we'd be manufacturing more millionaires over the next twenty years than the Industrial Revolution and Internet Boom combined.

How can it all mean ... nothing?

I think about people like David Crosswhite, a self-made man from humble beginnings who trusted us with millions of his dollars.

Now there's nothing left of it.

There are tens of thousands of others just like him, maybe more.

My nest egg is a bust too—at least the half of it I'd socked away in GenCoin.

The professor on the screen explains that there was a lot of "pumping and dumping" happening to artificially inflate the price and aside from that, an internal investigation found proof of embezzlement.

The host mentions that everything came to light all because of an anonymous whistleblower.

Reed.

It had to have been Reed.

And it makes perfect sense ...

The audit. The vagueness. Telling me not to take the job in New York. And finally, his explanation.

He had no choice.

He had no choice because he needed to do the right thing.

And he couldn't tell me because there was an active, federal-level investigation.

Grabbing my phone, I call him, only it goes straight to voicemail. I dial Lucy next, and she answers on the first ring.

"Oh, my God, Joa ..." she says.

"I know, I know. Hey, is Reed around today?"

"No. He left after our meeting this morning. Had a plane to catch."

Shit.

"How are you holding up? You feeling better?" she asks. "To be sick all week and then to wake up to this is just ... wow."

It hits me that I haven't so much as thought about the fact that I no longer have a job. I mean, it's a given, but I was too busy letting everything sink in to really give it much thought.

I'm jobless, but it's the least of my concerns because one of the best things to ever happen to me is sitting on an airplane with no idea how badly I want to throw my arms around him in this moment and tell him I forgive him.

I forgive him.

PAST

Joa

"But I don't understand how you can take an invisible Internet coin and suddenly tell me it's worth thousands of dollars." The husband half of the retired couple beside us at a little cafe in San Luis Obispo has been chatting up Reed for the past twenty minutes, Reed patiently explaining the concept of cryptocurrency not once, not twice, but three times, three different ways.

The man's wife glances my way with an apologetic smile before signing their check.

"It doesn't make sense!" The man pounds his fist on the table, causing the silverware to jump on dirty plates.

"Blockchains, Don," Reed says. "Blockchains."

"But where do you keep them? These coins?"

"In your wallet," Reed answers. "Your digital wallet. On the Internet. Where the coins are."

Don is red-faced, reaching for a glass of water before turning to his wife. "Pretty soon they're going to be telling us *the dollar bill is obsolete. Everyone's going to be using their invisible money. Let's hope to God we don't live long enough to see that day, Marian."*

"Don," she says, shooting him a look.

Reed and I chuckle to ourselves and exchange final pleasantries with the couple before they head out for their starlight boat tour.

"You were so patient with him," I say, reaching for my wine glass and hiding my smitten smile with a drink. "It was really sweet."

Reed rolls his eyes.

"You have a really good heart." I toss back the remains of my wine before stealing the bottle and pouring myself another glass.

It's getting chilly out here on the patio of Santiago's, but the gas lamp heaters that surround us take the bite out of the ocean wind.

"Tell me something I don't know," he teases.

I think I'm falling for you ...

26

REED

SHE DIDN'T CALL.

Maybe she's still sick.

Or maybe she's being stubborn.

Either way, she'll find out soon enough, if she hasn't already.

I take a sip of the gin and tonic the flight attendant mixed for me a few minutes ago—and I almost spit it out when I turn to my sister and see the ridiculous white blob she has on her face.

"What the hell is that?" I ask.

"A face mask." She pats it firmly against her skin, her eyes peeking out from two slits and her lips moving from behind another. "Planes can really dry out the skin, Reed. You want one? I think I have another ..."

"You look like a serial killer."

She winks. "You mean a serial killer with really great skin."

A few minutes later she peels the white blob from her face and rubs in the sticky remnants it left behind.

"See? I'm glowing," she says.

"No. You look like someone rubbed lube all over your face."

"You've been a real downer lately." She digs into her bag and pulls out a small, cobalt blue bottle of serum with a little eye dropper. Unscrewing the lid, she turns to me, "Just because you're pissed off at the world doesn't give you the right to take it out on everyone else."

"Bij, relax. It was a joke." I untangle the headphones in my lap. "Have I really been a downer lately?"

"Oh, my God, Reed. Yes." She slathers the blue oil on her face, rubbing it into her skin until it disappears. At twenty-six, my sister is far too obsessed with preserving her youth. I'm almost convinced she's beginning to age backwards, Benjamin Button-style. Pretty soon people are going to stop mistaking her for my girlfriend and start mistaking her for my daughter. "It's like ... you've been a different person this last year. I don't know. Something changed in you. You're not as fun as you used to be."

"Really?"

"Um, let's see. I invited you to Aspen back in February. You said you had to work. I invited you to a Red Hot Chili Peppers concert in March. You said you had to work. I invited you to Shay Mitchell's birthday party at Nobu and you said you had to work," she says. "And I've talked to your friends. They all say the same thing."

"When did you talk to my friends?"

"They follow me on Instagram. We message sometimes."

"Give me their names so I can kill them."

She rolls her eyes. "Anyway, you never want to do

anything anymore. You don't laugh like you used to. And anytime I'm with you, you're just this ... wet blanket."

"Thanks."

"You asked. I answered. Don't get mad."

"You waited a year to tell me this?" I ask.

"Champagne?" A flight attendant pushes a cart past our aisle.

"*Yass*, please," Bijou says, raising her hand like she's being called on in class. The flight attendant laughs as she hands her a crystal flute filled almost to the top with sparkling gold.

My sister is the queen of living in the moment.

I have to admit, it's one of the few things I actually envy about her.

"I had to tell a lot of people today that they no longer have jobs," I say, staring at the seatback before me.

"Ah. So that's what your deal is today," she says, taking a sip. "That blows."

"Part of it," I say.

"What's the other part?" She bats her faux lashes. "*A woman got you down?*"

I smirk at the way she says it, her chin tucked against her chest as she points at me.

"Oh, my God. I was just kidding," she says. "But I guess it makes sense. I mean, you were gone for days this week. You had to have been sleeping somewhere. And that girl you used to hook up with—what was her name? Joy-something? Didn't you tell me she transferred out here?"

I drag in a deep breath before confirming. "Yes. And her name is Joa. But honestly, Bij, I don't feel like talking about it right now."

She lifts a palm. "Fine. Your loss. But everyone says I give the best advice."

I'm not sure how that could be. Her life experience is akin to a spoiled toy poodle and the only boyfriends she's had was some guy from high school, a washed-up former boyband singer, and some sugar daddy she met on a dating app.

"Maybe some other time," I say, inserting my ear buds.

I browse through my downloaded podcasts before settling on The Tim Ferriss Show, but before I hit play, I turn to Bij and ask her one question.

"Do you ever want more for yourself?"

She looks up from the Us Weekly in her lap, her lips bent to the side like she's pondering my query.

Our childhood was one of luxury and privilege, and both of us are well aware of the fact that we're set for life. The only difference there is that I work by choice and she chooses not to work at all.

The world is in the palm of our hands.

Anything we want is ours.

But is that enough?

A man can't fuel his soul on worldly possessions alone.

"What, you mean like kids or something?" Bijou wrinkles her nose, as if the mere concept of future children disgusts her.

She's never been a big fan of anything that's noisy, smelly, or excessively needy. And when she was a kid, she never played with babies. Only Barbies. And none of the Barbies ever went on to have babies. They were too busy with their personal drama to start families of their own.

"I don't know," I say. "I just keep asking myself ... if the rest of my life was just like this, would that be okay?"

"Um, yes. That would be awesome. What kind of question is that?" Bijou scoffs.

"Why, are you unhappy or something?" she asks.

"I'm not unhappy. I just feel like something's missing."

Bijou flips a page in her magazine.

"It's that Joy girl," she says without hesitation.

"Joa," I correct her.

"She's what's missing. Or maybe you just need to get your rocks off. You were a lot happier when you were hooking up with her on the regular."

Bijou is the wrong person to get philosophical with. This is where Joa would come in handy. She was never afraid to talk about the bigger picture. In fact, I remember shutting down a lot of those conversations because she wasn't afraid to ask the big questions, the questions to which the truth was potentially terrifying.

Looking back, label or no label, we were in a relationship the entire time.

I was hers.

She was mine.

Even if we were both too stubborn and pigheaded to admit it.

As soon as this plane lands, I'm calling her.

This isn't over.

It never was.

PAST

Reed

Joa grips her sandwich with both hands, her legs crossed as she sits on a bench outside our office on her lunch break.

"Why are you eating your lunch out here?" *I ask as a city bus makes his presence known and leaves us in a cloud of exhaust.*

I wasn't looking for her, I just happened to notice her sitting here as I walked back from a client meeting a few blocks away.

"I almost always eat lunch out here. You didn't know that?" *she asks.*

Obviously not. She's worked here a hot minute. I don't know a damn thing about her other than the fact that when I'm not tearing her clothes off and claiming that pout of hers, I'm thinking about tearing her clothes off and claiming that pout of hers.

"Why?"

"All right. You caught me. I'm a closet people watcher,"

she says. "It's not as creepy as it sounds. I just find people interesting. That's all."

"So you sit here, eat your lunch, and stare at people."

"Basically." She takes a nibble of her sandwich. "Want to try?"

I smirk, taking a seat beside her.

"See that couple over there? Waiting for the bus? They break up every Monday. By Wednesday they're always back together. Tuesdays it's just her and she talks on the phone while she waits, so I usually get caught up on the drama then." She rolls her eyes. "So. Much. Drama."

"I don't understand the appeal of the whole boyfriend/girlfriend thing anymore," I say, watching the young couple scream at each other, arms flailing wildly and the girl looking like she's two seconds from snatching his phone from his hands and stomping it into bits. "I mean, unless you're looking for a one-way ticket to marriage and kids, there's really no point in dating. It's an outdated concept. Someday it'll be practically obsolete."

"Doubtful." She lifts a brow. "Love is a universal language. It brings people together. I'd hate to see what this world would look like without it."

"You think those two are in love?"

She chews her bite. "No. But I think they're too young and too busy fighting to realize it. They just think they are. But that? That's not love. That's entertainment."

We watch them a few minutes more, and then the city bus stops and they disappear inside.

"Have you ever been in love, Reed?" Joa asks, folding her sandwich wrapper in her lap.

"Random," I say. "But no, Joa. I haven't."

"Do you ever think you'll want that? For yourself? Someday?"

I lean forward, elbows resting on my knees and hands folded.

"I don't think about that kind of stuff," I say.

"Never?"

"Never." Turning to her, I say. "I don't need a girlfriend or love, Joa. I've got you."

"So basically I'm enabling your emotionally dysfunctional tendencies." Her words are dry. I can't tell if she's teasing or annoyed with me.

"Are you complaining? Pretty sure your end of the bargain isn't too shabby either."

Crumpling the wrapper, she gets up and tosses it in a nearby trashcan.

"Not complaining," she says as she eyes the main entrance to the building. "I just think it's kind of sad. Everyone should get to experience at least one great love in their life."

I stand, shoving my hands in my pockets and chuckling when she looks at me with pity in her eyes.

"Who knows," I say, "I've still got a lot of life ahead of me. Maybe it'll hit me when I least expect it. In the meantime, I'm not looking for it, and I'm sure as hell not sitting around feeling sorry for myself when I'm shacking up with you in tropical casitas."

"Fair enough."

I follow her inside and we wait for an elevator.

"What about you?" I ask. "Have you ever ...?"

Her pink lips dance a little. "Yes. I had a boyfriend in high school. We dated for three years until he went off to college. He was a year older than me. But he was my first love, and it was intense and magical and I wouldn't trade it for anything in the world."

Her hands clasp in front of her hips and her head tilts as she stares up at the ceiling with this dreamy, school-girl look on her face.

Heat flashes through me and my throat tenses.

Is that ...?

Did I ...?

Am I jealous?

I refuse to believe it, and by the time we get to our floor and go our separate ways, I don't give it another thought.

There's no way I'm jealous of her teenage ex-boyfriend.

Right?

27

Joa

I CHANGE INTO JEANS, grab a cardboard box, and gather my purse and keys. I'm heading into the office to clear out the rest of my belongings.

Lucy texted me a couple hours ago, said the FBI had raided the place, taking mostly files and computers. I have a few picture frames and smaller items I'd like to grab while I still have the chance.

I'm backing out of my driveway when my next-door neighbor waves for me to stop and makes her way across her side of the driveway to my passenger door.

"Hi, Agatha," I say, rolling the window down and lowering the volume on the radio. "What's going on?"

Her silvery hair is tucked into a stocking cap, and she wears a parka that makes her tiny frame look as though it doubled in size.

"I just wanted to see if that nice boy might be coming

around again anytime soon," she says, rosy cheeked and sparkle-eyed.

"Oh. Um. I'm not sure. Why do you ask?"

"I baked some thumbprint cookies. I wanted to give him a few as a thank you for the other day," she says. "My son and his family left last weekend. Went back home to Wisconsin Wednesday morning, I couldn't get my car to start. I knocked on your door to see if you were home and he answered. Long story short, he jumped my car with yours and shoveled both of our driveways."

"He did?"

"Sure did," she says, breath turning to clouds. "He's a keeper, that one. Reminds me so much of my Richard. God rest his soul."

She makes the sign of the cross before glancing up at the cloudless winter sky.

"If you see him again, tell him thank you for me," she says. "I simply cannot thank him enough."

"Of course." I nod and she trudges away in her snow gear, disappearing inside her garage.

I make my way to the train station, driving all the way in a foggy mental haze. Nothing about the past week and a half feels real, and the last four days are all but erased from my memory.

But it's the strangest thing.

I'm not even upset.

In fact, I've never felt more at peace.

———

THE OFFICE IS A WAR ZONE.

Pam dabs at teary eyes from behind her desk. From the

looks of it, she hasn't moved for a while. She's just sitting there, staring at a stack of Post-Its and an unplugged phone.

Passing by the first set of offices, I lose count of how many open and emptied file cabinets I find.

Did they think we're all in on this scam? What else are they looking for? I suppose they have to do a full and thorough investigation to make sure none of the innocent ones are roped into this and none of the guilty ones get out of this unscathed.

But still.

I get to my office and walk behind my desk. My computer tower is gone. Nothing but a gaping dark space and a bunch of lifeless cords.

Starting with my smaller drawers, I fish out all of my personal belongings. Chapsticks. Hand lotions. Travel-sized rollers of perfume. They've rifled through everything, but I manage to pluck out the things I need.

I move to the next drawer, then the next, but it's when I get to the fourth drawer that I gasp.

The little box with the silver wrapping paper and blue bow, the one Reed gave me that Christmas, is sitting in my bottom desk drawer, half covered with shuffled papers. A shiny contrast against a sea of white.

I threw this away.

I know I did.

He had to have fished it out of my waste paper basket after I left that day. Why didn't he say anything? When was he planning to give this to me?

"Oh, hey, you're here now." Lucy stands in my doorway. "What's that? Is that left over from the Secret Santa party?"

"No." I say, tugging at the bow until it unravels and falls onto the top of my desk. "It's from Reed."

Lucy comes closer, examining the small package in my hand.

"It's probably jewelry," she says. "That looks like a necklace box or something."

I carefully tear the paper and place it aside, revealing an unmarked, white cardboard box—the kind you might see at an arts and crafts fair.

"I bet it's a necklace. Or a bracelet," Lucy says.

The package feels heavier than a piece of jewelry would, and besides, we've never gifted each other anything. And at the time, we weren't dating. There'd have been no reason for him to buy me jewelry.

I slid the lid off the top and place it under the box.

It's a key.

Attached to a "Cabo is for Lovers" keychain he must have bought when we were in Cabo San Lucas together once. We had to have been hooking up for around six months by that point. I didn't even know he bought this.

I lift the keychain out of the box and notice a folded piece of paper beneath it. Unfolding the note, I hold my breath.

JOA,

What are we doing?

I'm crazy about you, and I know you feel the same.

Who are we trying to fool?

Reed

LUCY READS the note over my shoulder. "I don't get it."

"It's a key to his apartment." The cool metal rests in my palm and I read the lettering again. Cabo is for lovers. It's cheesy and I'm sure it cost him all of five dollars, but it's perfect. "We had this thing ... back when we were hooking up. Our apartments were off-limits to each other, no exceptions. This key ... this key means that I was more to him than just some hookup."

My eyes mist and dampen, but I blink it away.

I wish he was here right now.

"This is major, Lucy," I say. "You have no idea."

"So ... what now? Are you going to call him?"

Dangling the keys between us, I say, "No. I'm going to go see him."

PAST

Joa

If he doesn't hurry the hell up, I'm literally going to pee my pants.

My foot bounces as I wait in the passenger side of Reed's Range Rover. He picked me up for our weekend road trip, but we had to turn around because he forgot something.

The threat of sweat collects along my hairline, and I find myself scanning the perimeter to check out the bush situation.

And screw the no-visiting-each-other's-apartment rule. I'm making an executive decision and throwing it out the window right now.

But his building is massive, and while I know his apartment number, I don't think I could afford a wrong hallway.

I need a direct route, no wrong turns.

The pressure intensifies and my bladder throbs. According to the clock on the dash, he's been inside seven minutes now.

Grabbing my phone, I shoot him a text with three ques-tion marks, only to hear his phone vibrate in the console.

He left it behind.

Fanning myself, I squeeze my eyes and pray to God I don't burst right here in these beautiful, buttery leather seats.

The driver door opens a minute later, and Reed climbs in, tugging a baseball cap over his head. "Sorry about that."

We came back for a hat?

"You okay?" Worry lines sprout across his forehead, though I can hardly see them with his precious Dodgers cap in the way.

"Yeah, just ... can we stop at the 7-11 on the corner?" I ask.

He nods, backing out of the guest parking lot of his apart-ment complex and pulling onto the nearest street.

I can see the gas station from here. Green. Orange. Taunting.

Red light.

Reed slows to a stop and I take a deep breath.

"Seriously, Joa, are you all right?" he asks. "You look like you're uncomfortable or something."

The light turns green.

"Just go," I say, regretting those two giant bottles of water I drank this morning. I was trying to pre-hydrate myself for the weekend since I knew we'd be getting extra sun, but I wasn't planning for it to hit me all at once. "Unless you want me to wet myself."

Reed laughs, flooring the pedal and gunning us through the intersection—which makes things ten times worse for a hot second.

I don't wait for him to stop before I unfasten my seatbelt and open the passenger door. I'm sure I look like a lunatic sprinting for the door like this, but I don't have a choice.

When I get back, I feel halfway sane and all the way human again, and I hand him a package of Skittles I picked up on my way out.

"I would've let you use mine," he says.

"Just drive."

28

REED

IT'S BEEN a full twenty-four hours since I left Chicago. More than double that since I last saw Joa. I tried to call her as soon as I landed at LAX last night, but she didn't answer.

I thought about sending her a text, but desperate doesn't look good on anyone. Plus, she'll see the missed call. She'll know I was trying to reach out.

I just hope she doesn't think I had anything to do with the GenCoin scandal. So far, my name has been kept out of the media coverage. They've blasted Grosvenor's name and picture everywhere. Every news channel and media outlet and Internet site. Even though Coffey and Iaconelli were in on it, it's Grosvenor who's getting all the attention since he founded GenCoin and the pump-and-dump scheme was mostly his idea.

The asshole absolutely tried to pin it on me—forging emails and documents with my name on them and using my credentials to log into the different systems, but since I was working with the SEC, they assured me my name would be left out of everything and I'd be hailed as a hero when it was all said and done.

I heard from someone at the LA office that Grosvenor was escorted out by two men with federal badges on Friday.

God, I'd have loved to see that cocky bastard go down like that.

I merge onto the 405, heading home from a morning of running errands and finished with a little gym time and a hot shower.

My phone buzzes in my cupholder as I change lanes. I steal a quick glance the moment traffic comes to a standstill and read the message.

BIJOU: **Mom and Dad want to do a family dinner tonight. Martina is cooking!! She just got back from Paris!!**

A HALF HOUR LATER, I pull into the garage beneath my condo and head into the building, my gym bag slung over my shoulders as I text Bijou to let her know I'll be there.

Family dinners have never been my thing—at least not York family dinners—but I know it'd mean the world to my sister.

Plus Martina's cooking.

She was one of our full-time chefs growing up. Her husband got sick when I was about seventeen and she took some time off. Now she only cooks for us on special occasions or as requested.

I ride the elevator to the fifth floor and hop out, digging in my bag for my key.

The instant I'm in, I drop my wallet and keys on the entry console table before stopping dead in my tracks.

A lone suitcase in a familiar shade of olive-green rests in the middle of the living room. The place is quiet, but she's here. I can feel it.

Heading down the hallway, I notice my bedroom door is open a crack. I press my palm against the wood and it swings the rest of the way, revealing the most beautiful thing I think I've ever seen in my entire life perched on the foot of my bed.

"Joa ..."

"Nice place you've got here, York." Joa dangles the Cabo is for Lovers keyring in front of her face. Her baby blues gleam and she rises, sauntering my way. Her hands glide over my shoulders the second we connect.

Her lips graze mine, teasing me, and I lift her into my arms, wrapping her legs around my sides as I carry her to my bed.

"I'm going to tell you everything," I whisper. "This past year was brutal ... not being able to explain, to give you the explanation you deserved. To know that you hated me for what you thought I did."

Though I'm well aware of the fact that she's a highly intelligent creature and odds are she's already pieced everything together by now.

She silences me, her finger pressed against my mouth as if to say, "Not now."

I place her on the bed. Hovering above her, I brace myself with one arm while the other hand works the button of her jeans.

Our lips meet, hungry and impatient, as we remove our clothes until there's nothing left but the two of us.

"This," I say, wearing a smirk as I pull her into my lap. "This is how it was always supposed to be."

"Naked in bed?" she asks.

I shoot her a look. "No. You in my bed, in my apartment, with me."

Her pretty lips bend at the corners and she presses her smile against mine until it turns into a kiss. Our tongues dance, our fingers interlace, and she grinds against me like the teasing little minx she's always been.

My cock throbs until it aches. I've never wanted to be inside of her more than I do in this moment. All the times before this, as mind-blowing as they were, won't hold a shadow to all the things I'm about to do to her now.

Rising on her knees, she reaches between her spread legs and wraps her palm around my shaft, pumping the length before positioning it at her slit.

Everything holds in this moment. Our stares. Our eyes. Our tongues. And then she lowers herself onto me, head rolling back as she exhales.

I cup the side of her jaw, pulling her closer to me and peppering feverish kisses into her neck and collarbone as her hips buck and circle.

There's no rhythm here.

There's no method to our madness.

I want what I want and she wants what she wants.

It's a goddamned free-for-all.

I gather her hair in my fist as she rides me, and every time she bites into her lower lip I get a little harder.

Her perfect teardrop breasts bounce with every breathless plunge of her body onto mine.

When her hand squeezes the back of my arm, I know

she's getting close. While I could do this all night, it's in this moment I have to remind myself Joa Jolivet isn't going anywhere.

Not this time.

Not ever again.

PAST

Reed

"That's not the suitcase you brought with you, right?" I ask as she packs up her things after a three-day stint in Portland. "Pretty sure I'd remember an eyesore like that."

"Hey." She shoots me a look as she folds a t-shirt and places it inside.

"Seriously though, where did you get that? And when?"

"I got it at the flea market this morning when you were out for a run. It's vintage. A Ventura."

"What's wrong with the black Samsonite you came with?"

"Nothing." She shrugs. I'm still confused as to why she would swap out her perfectly good, perfectly modern and practical luggage for something that looks like it fell off some VW bus in 1973. She shuts the lid and snaps the locks. "When I was a kid, my parents had luggage just like this. Hand-me-downs from my mom's parents. Every time my parents would go away for a weekend, they'd pack their things in a bag just like this, but they'd always leave extra room so they could bring us back something."

The sweetest smile claims her lips as she reminisces.

"Anyway, I know you don't care, so I won't bore you with the rest of the story," she adds, sliding the thing off the bed and placing it in the corner.

"There's more?" I ask as she scans the room in search of anything she may have left behind.

Her light eyes lift to mine and she winks. "There's always more. But I know it's not your thing, so no worries. Phone charger. That's what I'm forgetting."

She's already out the door and down the hall before I realize there's a part of me that wants to hear the rest of the story.

29

Joa

"THANK you so much for having me, Mrs. York." I shake his mother's hand Saturday night as we stand in the entrance of the Yorks' Malibu mansion.

I have to admit it's difficult looking her in the eyes, knowing what I know. Knowing how she abandoned Reed in hotel rooms as a small child. Knowing how he spent his entire life as an afterthought. But those things are none of my business, and if Reed's made peace with his past, I have to accept that. Maybe someday I can get him to open up a little more. I imagine he's kept most of it bottled up his entire life.

But for now, he's asked me to meet his parents, and so I'm here—with proverbial bells on.

The house smells of fresh, salted air, baked sand, and a hint of coconut sun tan oil, and I'm pretty sure there are more windows here than there are in all of Mills Haven, but I try not to get distracted.

There'll be time to gawk later, I'm sure.

"It's our pleasure, darling. And please, call me Bebe," she says, tucking her white-blonde hair behind one ear. A giant pearl surrounded by a cluster of diamonds sparkles in the late-afternoon sun. "It isn't every day that my son brings along a ... *friend.*"

She smiles when she says the word, "friend." And then she winks at Reed.

"What my sweet mother is trying to say is that it's kind of a big deal that you're here." Bijou, Reed's younger sister chimes in. She's the spitting image of her mother, head-to-toe, only about thirty years younger.

So far I've only talked to her for about fifteen minutes at Reed's and then in the car on the drive out here. Before I met her, Reed warned me that she was an "acquired taste." But I find her hilarious, the way she says what's on her mind and doesn't give a damn what anyone thinks. She isn't afraid to be herself, even calling herself a "Malibu Barbie Basic Bitch."

She owns it.

And to that I say: more power to her.

"Why don't you all come in and get settled. Martina should have the food out shortly. She's been cooking all afternoon." Bebe diverts down a long hallway. "Redford? Are you in your study, darling?"

Reed hooks his hand into the bend of my elbow, leading me to a dining room. The table in the center is fit for royalty, covered in matching china and a crystal candelabra. But despite the elegance, the entire home still offers a modern, coastal vibe.

Outside the windows, the waves crash on the shore. Reed said if it wasn't so chilly, we'd be eating on the patio tonight. I told him sixty-eight degrees wasn't chilly to a

Midwesterner. He told me I'd be more than welcome to sit out there, but I'd be dining solo.

Reed pulls a chair for me before taking the one next to it. Bijou sits across from us, checking her reflection in her phone's camera.

Bebe glides into the room, her long Pucci dress billowing around her when she walks, and she takes a seat between Reed and his sister.

"It's so nice that we could all get together tonight," she says, hands clasped as she beams at her grown children. "And Joa, I very much look forward to getting to know you."

"Hey, Dad." Bijou puts her phone away as her father takes a seat. "How was vacay?"

"Good, good." He glances my way, and I'm sure he finds it weird that his son suddenly and randomly brought a woman over to meet them.

A woman in a white chef's coat with a slick gray bun carries a tray toward us, making her way around the table and delivering small bowls of some kind of bisque.

Bebe and Redford share stories from their latest trip before diving into plans for the next one—they're thinking Grenada next time.

Bijou shares an embarrassing story about Reed—something about the time he lost a bet and she put makeup on him and made him answer the door when the pizza delivery guy arrived.

Between courses, Reed reaches under the table, squeezing the top of my knee or slipping his fingers between mine.

When we're finished, Bebe and Redford escape to his study for a cocktail and Bijou plants herself on the sofa in the family room, her nose in her phone.

"You keep looking at the ocean," Reed says when it's

just us and we're sitting at a table that's long since been cleared.

"I just can't imagine growing up like this."

He laughs. "I didn't grow up here. We actually lived in a house a couple miles up the coast. It was about half the size of this."

My eyes widen. Half the size of this place would still be ten times the size of the house I grew up in.

"Most parents downsize when their kids move out. Not mine. They do everything backwards," he says. "Kind of like how most couples travel the world before they have kids? Yeah, not mine."

"I still find all of this fascinating." I glance around the dining room, which is essentially three walls of windows with a panoramic ocean view. "I hope your parents never take for granted how beautiful this is."

"Oh. They do." He gets up from the table, placing his hand out.

I slip my palm into his and he pulls me to a standing position. "Where are we going?"

"You want to walk the beach a little bit?"

I scan the view past the back patio, where a glowing moon reflects on a dark and rippling ocean.

"I thought you said it was too chilly," I say.

"It absolutely is. But I'm willing to freeze my ass off because that's the kind of guy I am."

He's trying to be a smart ass, but I don't care. I'm smitten. Helplessly and instantly obsessed, straddling the line between wanting to rush full speed ahead into this new life with him and begging for time to stand still so I can savor these moments as they come.

Reed leads me through the living room, where he yanks

a very expensive-looking blanket from the back of a sofa and wraps it around my shoulders.

We pass through a sliding glass door next, kicking off our shoes and abandoning them on the patio steps as we race toward the mild evening waves that roll against the shore.

I almost beat him until he catches up with me, wrapping his arms around me and tackling me to the ground.

He hovers above me, and I place my hands on his arms. His skin is freezing already. I suppose it gets colder quicker here by the ocean.

"You're ice cold," I say, sitting up and pulling the blanket out from beneath me. "Here. We can share."

Reed kisses me, slow and lingering, the taste of red wine still on his mouth.

"I like your family," I tell him. "They're a riot."

"To put it nicely."

"I love how your mother calls everyone 'darling.' And your sister just calls it like she sees it. Your dad, I'm still trying to get a read on him, but he seems like the kind that might loosen up with a good cigar and a few drinks in him."

"You're very perceptive," he says. "And absolutely correct. Though you forgot to throw in some Cuban music. The man goes nuts when Buena Vista Social Club comes on. Pretty sure he was Cuban in a past life."

"What do you think you were in a past life?" I ask.

He makes a face.

"You don't have to believe in past lives. This is purely a hypothetical question for my entertainment only," I assure him.

He mulls it over for a minute, as if there's some kind of right or wrong answer.

"A saint," he finally says.

"A saint?"

"Yeah. Pretty sure I did something amazing in my past life to deserve the life I have now," he says. "What about you?"

"I was going to say Viking goddess or something, but I don't think I can top that, York."

I quiet his laugh with a kiss and ignore the threat of shivers that pass through me each time the wind gusts.

I don't want to go inside.

I don't want this night to end.

I want to stay here, like this, with him, and not have a single care in the world ... forever.

"Where do we go from here?" I ask him.

He stares toward the water, eyes narrowing. "I don't know. Thought maybe we could open our own consultancy? Maybe specialize in cryptocurrency fraud or something? You wouldn't believe everything I learned over the last year. Seems like it'd be a waste not to do anything with it."

I chuckle, placing a hand across his chest. "No. I mean where do we go from here as in ... you and me?"

His diamond blues light when he looks at me, sending a tingle that moves from my middle to the top of my head.

"Anywhere you want to go, Joa," he answers. "You've got me. I'm with you."

30

REED

I SWEAR I just saw my whole life flash before my eyes.

Joa sits at my kitchen island, wearing one of my white button downs, reading the news on my iPad, and drinking coffee from my favorite mug.

She's been here a week now, which is definitely a record and deserves some kind of trophy or medal or at the very least a certificate of achievement signed by me personally. Framed and matted of course.

Many have tried.

None of succeeded.

Until now.

Before Joa, if I brought a girl here, she'd be lucky to see the inside of my place for more than a few hours. And I never let them stay over. Always had some excuse at the ready about why they had to leave.

But it's different now.

A little part of me dies if she wakes up before me. And

if she runs out to check the mailbox because she's bored and wants to be helpful, that's five minutes of me missing her.

I'm pathetic, but at least I own it.

And besides, I wouldn't have it any other way.

I'd rather be lovesick than the so-called wet blanket that I've been for the past year.

"You about done staring over there?" Joa asks, looking up from her screen. "By my count, that was a solid three minutes. Any longer and I might start to worry."

"Can't a man admire his sexy girlfriend without getting any guff?"

Her smile fades.

We hadn't had this discussion yet.

We've never used labels.

For the longest time they were taboo, practically verbal contraband.

"I'm your *girlfriend*?" she asks, sliding off the bar stool and lacing her fingers around my favorite mug as she slinks toward me. "I thought you hated that word."

"I used to hate it," I say. "That was before I decided it was useful."

"Useful how? Exactly?"

"Mostly, you know, in social situations. When I'm introducing you to people," I say. "It's a subtle way to say 'she's mine, so back the hell off because you don't have a chance in hell.'"

Her rosebud lips contain a smirk. "You got all that from one little word?"

"Yep."

"Impressive." She lifts her arm over my shoulder, hooking her hand around the back of my neck. "I was thinking about what you said last week. About starting our own consultancy."

"Yeah?"

"I think we should do it. Let's go for it." Her eyes smile and she's nodding her head like a kid who's just been asked if she wants to go to Disneyland, but she's also scared as hell. I see it beneath the excitement. "E-currency fraud and security. We could rock the hell out of that. And we could travel the world, work from anywhere we want. Just a couple of restless souls doing what they do best and getting paid for it at the same time."

God, I still can't believe she's here, standing in my kitchen, wearing my shirt and nothing else, talking about plans for a future with me.

I don't know how I got so lucky, but I vow never to take her for granted so long as I live.

I know what it's like to lose her, and I'd rather die a hundred deaths than experience that darkness again.

31

Joa

ONE MONTH LATER ...

REED STEADIES his arm around my shoulders as we stand atop a cliff that overlooks the bluest waters I've ever seen accented with an azure sky and white-washed cubi-form houses built into the natural landscape.

Santorini is paradise on earth. Devastatingly gorgeous.

I rest my head against his shoulder, nestling it just beneath his chin, and he holds me tight. The gentle wind rustles my hair and kisses my face, and it carries with it the scent of the sea.

For the past five weeks, I've been staying mostly in LA, trekking back to Chicago every couple of weeks to take care of things back home.

Every time I return to Mills Haven, Reed insists on joining me. At first I thought it was simply because he's crazy in love with me and just can't get enough—then I saw the light.

My family adores him in a borderline-obsessive kind of way. Every time he comes around, they shower him with attention, make him the center of the conversation, and hug him at least three times before we leave.

Mom gets a kick out of making him try her various family casserole recipes and Dad loves to geek out with him and talk numbers.

And last time we were home, Logan and Reed discovered they both played intramural rugby at the state level and they're both MLB fans, so now that's all they talk about.

Between those three and Neve and the twins, Reed struggles to divide his time fairly, but I never hear him complain.

The few times I've spent with his family over the past month have been enjoyable but also on the superficial side. Conversation is kept light and shallow, never delving into any remotely deep topics. Their interactions are filled with meaningless formalities. Lots of "How have you beens" and "fines" and never any elaborations.

My heart squeezes when I think of Reed as a child, probably starved for love and attention, never knowing what it felt to be loved in a deeper-than-the-ocean kind of way that defies logic and requires no conditions.

It truly is amazing, the man he turned out to be.

All this time, I mistook his guardedness for arrogance. I had him pegged all wrong. He just hadn't let his walls down yet.

"Let's stay here forever," I say to Reed. We've been here seven nights and six days and we're supposed to leave tomorrow. It was only meant to be a quick getaway. We still have an insane amount of work to do back home to get our business off the ground.

"We'll be back. Someday." He squints into the Aegean Sea. "Maybe we'll pull a Redford and Bebe and come back here solo *after* we have kids."

He's never mentioned kids.

Hell, he's never mentioned marriage or anything that spans beyond the rest of this year unless it pertains to our private corporation.

"I was kidding," he says. "We'll bring them with us, of course."

"I never knew you wanted kids."

"Yeah. Me neither," he says. "Until I met you."

Reed turns me to face him and brushes a windblown strand of hair away from my face. His mouth skims against mine.

"I love you, Joa," he says. "I've loved you from the start— I just didn't know it at the time. I didn't know what love was until I met you."

I let his words sink into the deepest parts of me before locking them away forever.

"I love you too." I rise on my toes and kiss him, and in this moment I know.

He's the man I'm going to spend the rest of my life with.

EPILOGUE

REED

FIVE YEARS LATER ...

"HAPPY BIRTHDAY, DEAR KAIA ..."

Our one-year-old daughter squirms in her high chair as my wife watches the flickering candle like a hawk, ready to pounce should anything go awry.

The gang's all here. Tom and Bevin, Neve, Cole, Emmeline, Ellison, and baby Evan, Logan and his new fiancé, Michaela, Bijou and my parents. Even Lucy made the trek out here to Mills Haven to celebrate our daughter's first birthday.

The song finishes, and Joa helps Kaia blow out her candle. Everyone claps, including Kaia. A minute later, she's double fisting her vanilla smash cake with pink frosting, shoving it into her mouth until her cheeks look as if they could explode.

When she's finished, her face is stained pink from the frosting and her dark hair is highlighted with white cake crumbs.

I head out to the patio to check on the grill situation.

It's so weird to be one of *those* guys. The ones with the house in the suburbs. The ones who test drive minivans and dream about coaching their kids' soccer teams when the time comes.

Three years ago, I married the love of my life.

Two years ago, we started trying for a baby—which happened a lot sooner than we expected.

And a year ago, shortly after Kaia arrived, we moved to Mills Haven to be closer to family. My parents are travel fiends and assured us they would be happy to make the trek to Chicago on a regular basis, and Joa's parents are so hands-on and willing to help it just seemed like the right decision.

Our business does well enough that we can be choosy about our clientele, only opting to take on the contracts that fit into our schedule.

From outside, I watch through the sliding door as Joa wipes Kaia's hands and face with a damp washcloth. Joa's saying something, shaking her head and laughing, and Kaia's dimples flash.

Motherhood came natural to her. Probably helps that her own mother was Super Mom incarnate. One of my favorite things is to listen on the baby monitor on the nights when Joa puts Kaia to bed.

She sings her Raffi songs.

Reads her Dr. Seuss books.

Tells her the most ridiculous stories she makes up on the fly.

I couldn't have picked a better mother for my child, and already I can't wait until the next one and the next one.

I want that crazy, loud house filled with kids and laughter and cheesy traditions. I want to be the dad that dresses in matching superhero costumes with his kids on Halloween, the one who chaperones field trips and mows his own lawn in the summer. I want to be the husband who isn't afraid to kiss his wife in front of their kids, so their kids can know what true love looks like.

It won't always be perfect.

It won't always be magical.

But it will be filled with love and a bond that can never be severed no matter what may come our way. Real love never ends, never goes away.

Joa taught me that.

Chapter 1

Aerin

"With all due respect, Mr. Welles, I'm not understanding the scope of this contract." My back is arrow-straight, my legs are crossed at the knees, and my hands are folded in my lap despite the fact that we're FaceTiming and he can't see anything lower than my cardigan-covered shoulders. The five-page agreement his assistant emailed me this morning is stacked in a neat pile to my right. "You want me to provide concierge ministrations for your son? And what does he do, exactly? Just trying to get an idea of what kind of services I'd be providing."

I spent hours last night Googling Calder Welles and his twenty-eight-year-old namesake, Calder Welles II. At one point, I must have had thirty tabs open in my browser.

According to the uber-reliable source that is Wikipedia,

the elder Calder Welles is the president and CEO of WellesTech, a technological conglomerate that also owns a news network and one of the most popular video on-demand streaming services in the world.

His mysterious son, however? His Internet existence seems to be boiled down to a couple of lines in his father's WellesTech website biography. He might as well be fictional. I couldn't so much as find a single photograph of him that was a) recent and b) unblurred.

He has inky dark hair.

That's about all two solid hours of online research could give me.

Mr. Welles leans forward in his russet-colored chair and clears his throat. "My son ... is a bit of a ... free spirit. With an extremely difficult ... disposition. To put it nicely."

I'm still confused. "Does he work with you? At WellesTech?"

I already know the answer. According to the Welles-Tech staff directory, the only Calder Welles who works there is the one on the other side of this screen.

His lips pull at the sides, revealing a too-perfect smile that contrasts against his tawny, wrinkled skin.

Veneers.

Definitely veneers.

"Not exactly," he says with a slight chuckle that morphs into a sputtering cough. "But that's the goal. That's why I'm hiring you."

I haven't agreed to sign the contract, but I won't mention that yet.

Over the past three years, I've concierge'd for Silicon Valley executives, Fortune 500 CEOs, Hollywood royalty, and Orange County stay-at-home wives, and while they ran the gamut as far as personality quirks and backgrounds, the one thing they all had in common was that they needed me. They had work for me to do. I was hired to make their busy, chaotic lives easier. All of my charges know that if they hire me, they have absolutely nothing to worry about. I'm a self-starter. If I need an answer to something, I find it without bothering them. I'm resourceful and quick on my feet. The most responsible woman they'll ever know.

They call me "the control freak's answer to a personal assistant," and for that reason and that reason alone, I've got a client wait list five miles long.

"I'll be stepping down in the coming year." He lifts a veiny fist to his thin lips, wheezing until he manages to wrangle the narrow glass of water in front of him. "And I'd like to get my ducks in a row, so to speak."

"So he's taking over the company and you're hiring me to make his life easier while you train him?" I ask, resisting the urge to reorganize the pens in my pencil cup by color and tip size. Instead, I slide the cup behind my monitor.

Out of sight, out of mind.

Works every time.

"He hasn't agreed. Not yet," Mr. Welles says. "Let's just say we're not exactly on speaking terms."

He's crazy.

This man is certifiably insane.

And I should've known that after reading his Wiki bio. Mr. Welles has been married four times, owns eleven homes all over the world, a fleet of vintage Italian sports cars, a mega yacht named *My Way*, a 24k gold iPhone, and a lock of Elvis Presley's hair. Of course he thinks he can bribe his son to take over his company by providing him with a personal concierge.

Makes perfect sense ... if you're missing a few screws.

"I'm so sorry, Mr. Welles," I say to a man who is clearly

used to getting everything he wants. "I'm not sure I'm what you're looking for."

Had he read my curriculum vitae in full detail, he'd know this.

I provide personal assistance for persnickety types. I run errands. I organize closets. I schedule travel. I coordinate projects. I walk dogs. I pay bills. I grocery shop. I schedule spa visits. I've even given foot massages, made allergy-friendly school bake sale cookies, and once flew on a private jet to Paris to pick up a special order Birkin for a US senator's wife. My job isn't glamorous or prestigious by any means, but I'm good at what I do. Correction: amazing at what I do.

But being hired by an eccentric billionaire to assist his estranged son doing ... what, I'm not sure ... that's a first. The son clearly doesn't want or need me, and I'd rather be productive and stay busy than follow someone around like an unwanted pet, waiting for him to throw me a bone.

"Of course you are." His chest puffs and his mouth curves down. I've offended him.

"I'm sure there are thousands of personal assistants in New York," I say, eyeing the clock on the wall. I have three more FaceTime interviews lined up after this and a full inbox screaming for my attention. The number thirty-eight waits impatiently in that tiny red circle, taunting me.

"I've been told you're the best." His brows meet.

My ego purrs like a contented kitten on the inside, but I contain myself. "I appreciate that you're discerning in who you hire, Mr. Welles, but I'm afraid I've got a wait list and at this point in my career, I'm being particularly judicious with my commitments."

"One hundred thousand per month," he says.

If I had coffee in my mouth, I'd spit it out right now. That's over four times my going rate.

He's lost his damn mind.

I respond with silence, my mind too busy running quick tabulations on what I could do with that kind of money. My student loans? Gone. Down payment on a condo? Boom. A real vacation? Costa Rica, here I come.

"Three hundred," he says. Clearly he mistook my stunned silence for something else.

"Mr. Welles—"

"Ms. Keane," he cuts me off. "Perhaps I should make myself a little clearer: I'm dying. I don't have a lot of time left. My son won't speak to me. I need a middleman. Someone who can help me get through to him."

I was afraid of this ...

"I'm so sorry to hear that, Mr. Welles. Forgive me for asking, but if you're not on speaking terms, how do you know he needs or even wants a concierge?" I ask. In my mind, I imagine myself turning down other jobs, hopping on a plane to New York, and having Calder Welles *the Second* laugh in my face and refuse my services.

He'd have every right, too.

"That's for me to worry about, Ms. Keane." His chin juts forward and he straightens his emerald-striped tie. "So what do you say? Three hundred thousand for the month?"

"And what if he doesn't need me for the entirety of the month?" I ask.

"You'll be paid the same whether you work one day or thirty."

I couldn't say 'no' to that offer if I wanted to.

Licking my lips, I sit a little straighter and pull in a long breath before letting it go.

"All right, Mr. Welles," I say. "I accept your offer."

My track record is perfect, which has contributed to the word-of-mouth, near-overnight success I've known the last few years.

I'm a workaholic perfectionist who's *never* made a mistake.

But something tells me ... that's all about to change.

Chapter 2

Calder

"Your phone's going off." There's a woman's voice in my ear followed by the slip of a delicate arm beneath mine. A nose nuzzles against the bend of my neck a moment later, breath warm and soft on the top of my shoulder.

Normally I'm adept at weeding out the sea barnacles, but evidently my gauge was off last night.

"Babe, someone's calling you ..." she whispers into my ear again, and I shudder.

Babe?

We met last night.

My lips begin to part, the instructions to, "*Don't ever call me that again,*" on the edge of my tongue, but her hand slides down my chest, and a moment later her long skinny fingers are wrapped around my morning wood. "You want me to silence it for you?"

I sense a wicked grin in her soft voice, and while I'm not the biggest fan of reheating leftovers, she has me in a particularly vulnerable position.

"I should get this. I'm expecting an important call," I lie. Her warm hand unpries from my cock and she slinks back to her side of the king-sized bed. In the dark and from the corner of my eye, I watch her pull the sheets against her chest, tucking them under her arms like a makeshift towel.

Oh, *now* she wants to be shy?

I reach for the phone and flip it over to see who the hell is bothering me at six twenty-one in the morning, but the number flashing on my screen isn't a number at all.

It's three words.

All caps.

DO NOT ANSWER.

The girl in my bed watches me, our eyes catching before her gaze flicks away. She's curious, I'm sure. Women always are, especially when they've tasted hope in the form of sexual attention and multiple orgasms. She's probably wondering who could possibly be so important that I'd snuff out another round with her perfect, pointed C-cups and Angelina Jolie mouth.

I won't deny the physical chemistry we shared last night, but she'd be a damn fool to believe she's any different from any other woman I've devoured in my day.

Against my better judgement—and because I've already committed to answering the call in front of my present company—I press the pad of my thumb against the green circle and exhale.

A second later, I answer with a cold and curt, "Hello?"

"Calder?" It's a woman's voice.

Not what I expected.

"Who is this?" I glance at the caller ID on my phone again, half wondering if I was dreaming those three little words before.

"Marta." She states her name like a question. "Marta McDaniel."

Oh.

Right.

My father's assistant.

I've seen her name at the bottom of those letters he used to send me. What kind of man dictates his personal business and has his secretary transcribe them?

Calder Welles Senior. That's who.

I pull the glass screen away from my ear, half-tempted to press the red button and put us both out of our misery right this instant.

I haven't heard from the bastard in four years—after I told him off for the ninth time. I'm saving the tenth and final time for the day that sorry excuse for a man is lying helpless, frail, alone, and unloved on his deathbed—which I'm sure will be a Duxiana mattress covered in thousand thread count sheets because only the best will do for a man who has everything.

"I'm so sorry to bother you, but your father needs to set up a meeting with you as soon as possible," she says.

Needs.

That's rich.

I have needs too, Marta, I want to tell her. *Needs that have never meant a fucking thing to the narcissistic pig who named his one and only son after himself, only to spend decades pretending he didn't exist. Amongst other atrocities.*

"I'm afraid I'm busy," I say.

It's not a lie. I have a life. One that doesn't involve that selfish old bastard and his shiny bald head and beady eyes and those papery, wrinkled hands he never could keep to himself for more than five minutes at a time.

Just ask my childhood nanny, a perky college coed who had no idea what she was signing up for by agreeing to work for the Welles family.

Or the striking, honey-skinned Puerto Rican house-keeper he hired.

And my mother's hospice nurse ... *Brittany* — who subsequently went on to become the second (but not the last) Mrs. Welles, a marriage that lasted a mere two-hundred and forty-six days.

"Of course," Marta says, her voice colored in gentle persuasion. I've never met Marta (and never intend to), but her jovial voice reminds me of a pleasantly plump Midwestern grandmother with wavy silver hair and chunky jewelry that she couples with bedazzled sweater sets. I picture her work desk littered with pictures of her extended family, each photo ambiguous enough to silently persuade others to ask where she fits into the mix, just so she has an excuse to talk about her family.

If I'm right about her, Marta would be the first secre-tary my father has had in decades who didn't come equipped with fake breasts and a too-eager-to-please mentality.

But all of this is one hundred percent based on prob-ability.

I haven't seen the self-centered mogul since my eigh-teenth birthday, when his wife (at the time) insisted on throwing a graduation party more befitting for a child finishing kindergarten than a strapping eighteen-year-old man child who spent the majority of his teenage years counting down the days until he could get the hell out of

Bridgeforth Military Academy—the well-to-do's private version of juvenile detention.

The only crime I ever committed was being born the first, last, and only son of Calder Hereford Welles.

Guilty. But not of my own volition.

A gorgeous gypsy-looking woman in Rome pulled me aside at a bar several years ago, told me she "knew things," and then proceeded to tell me I was a reincarnation of a fifteenth-century prince, and that I chose the life I have now because I needed to exact revenge on someone who wronged me in that life.

I think she was full of shit, but I liked the idea of what she said.

"I understand," Marta hums a little before she speaks again. I must make her nervous. "But as I said, it's extremely urgent. He wouldn't bother you if it wasn't."

Right.

The girl in my bed, whose name suddenly escapes me, stares dead-eyed at her phone screen, the bright light illuminating her face as she scrolls with the methodical mechanics of a robot.

I don't know much about her, other than what she told me over drinks at the hotel bar last night. She's a drug rep from Minnesota, here for a medical conference, and she's the youngest of seven. Catholic if I recall correctly. She made a point in telling me her parents didn't believe in birth control. My expression must have ashened when she told me that because she immediately proceeded to reach into her purse and pull out a pale pink compact filled with birth control pills. I responded by reaching into my wallet and retrieving a magnum-sized rubber.

"Calder?" Marta's voice brings me back to the present moment. "Still there?"

"Yes." I pinch the bridge of my nose before rubbing the sleep from my eyes, and then I release a heavy breath into the phone. "I'll have my assistant get a hold of you. Set something up."

Marta is quiet. "You ...you don't have an assistant."

"A lot has changed in four years, Marta," I'm quick on the reply.

She clears her throat, quiet. "All right, then. May I have her number? I'd be happy to reach out first."

"I'll forward her your contact information. She'll be in touch."

Marta's nervous humming fills the ear piece, a cross between a laugh and a two-note song. That little quirk would get old quickly if she were my assistant. But I won't have to worry about that. I'm never going to have an assistant. The idea of having to talk to and look at the same person day in and day out is about as appealing as gouging my eyes out with rusty pliers.

I crave change.

I crave variety.

I crave a tether-free existence where I rely on no one but myself.

Anything else would be a prison sentence.

"I would love to have her email at least," Marta says, her voice slightly shaky. "If that's all right with you."

I imagine my father standing over her, clinging on to her every word, scribbling shaky notes onto Post-Its with his weighty gold pen, micromanaging every sentence that comes out of her thin-lipped mouth because the man is obsessed with my approval ...

I'm the only person on this entire planet he can't pay, manipulate, or scheme into respecting him. But respect is the one thing he'll never have from me until his dying day, and even then, when his shriveled, lifeless body rots, encased in the family mausoleum in Bedford, he still won't have it.

But I'll be there.

I'll be there to remind him what a piece of shit he is as he takes his last breath, and I'll be there to spit on his grave as the concrete is sealed.

A bittersweet and just finality fitting for an asshole of my father's caliber.

"Calder ... I don't know how to tell you this, so I'm just going to say it." Marta is quiet for a second, a dramatic pause perhaps, likely my old man's suggestion. "Your father is dying."

The girl in my bed is still scrolling through her Instagram feed. I don't even think she's fucking blinked in the last two minutes.

Hannah.

That's her name.

Not that it matters.

"Calder, your father is—" she begins to speak again, her voice an octave higher and a notch louder.

"—I heard you the first time." My voice booms enough that Hannah's shiny eyes dart up and her phone almost drops from her hand.

"He'd like to meet with you to discuss matters of his estate," she says.

"I'm sure he has a will." Not that I want anything from him. Money—and the Welles name—is nothing more than a burden. "And I'm certain that when the time comes, his attorney will be in contact with me."

"There are some matters he'd like to discuss with you personally—while he's still able," she says. "The meeting won't take long. Maybe ten or fifteen minutes of your time is all. Could you come by this afternoon? Your father has time between one fifteen and one forty-five."

"Not going to happen," I say. I'm in Telluride, enjoying an impromptu weekend of skiing and snowboarding. Or at least ... I *was* enjoying it.

I move to the edge of the bed, my back folded and my forehead pressed against my open palm. The keys to my Cessna lie on my nightstand. I could fly back to the city today if I wanted to.

If I wanted to ...

My father wanting to "go over matters of his estate" is nothing more than code for him wanting to manipulate me into doing something he wants me to do ... something that would benefit him because it's always about him even when he's supposedly dying.

As far as I'm concerned, there's nothing he's holding over me in this moment, and that makes me a free man. There's not enough Welles money in the world to make me want to change that.

The girl in my bed slinks out from beneath the covers before fishing around on the floor for last night's clothes—a skintight lace dress if memory serves me.

"Calder ... do you have a phone charger?" she whispers, wincing as if she's sorry for bothering me during my *important* phone call.

"Marta, I have to let you go," I say.

My father's assistant begins to protest, but it's too late. I've already hit the red button.

I have to admit ... my curiosity is piqued, and telling my father off one last time before he croaks is on my proverbial bucket list, but I won't be had that easily.

If I decide to show up, it'll be on my own time. And only if I feel like it.

I drop my phone into the mess of covers and sheets before dragging a hand down my tired face. A second later, I swipe my boxers off the floor and pull them on.

"Everything okay?" she asks.

"Yeah." I rest my hands on my hips, trying to figure out a way to tell Hannah she can't use my phone charger because it's time for her to go.

"Did you want to grab breakfast downstairs?" The girl reaches behind her back with impressive flexibility to get her zipper. She must do yoga. "The lounge here has the best blueberry waffles."

"I don't eat breakfast." I lie. I eat breakfast, just not with nameless women I pick up in hotel bars. Every hook up serves a purpose, and her work here is done.

Stepping into her heels, she simultaneously runs a hand down the front of her wrinkled dress to smooth out a crease. "That's too bad."

In the dark of the room, she manages to locate her bag, and she slips her nearly-dead phone inside.

I wait until she's finished dressing before I walk her to the door.

"I'm here until Friday," she says, her hand on the door lever and a hint of hope in her voice. "Room 211."

Hannah gives a timid smile, one that wholly contradicts all the wild and kinky things she did to me mere hours ago, and I *almost* feel bad.

There's a Midwestern wholesomeness about her, a glimmer of hope in her pale eyes, and a naive sweetness in the way she looks at me, her mouth curled in a half-smile.

But this doesn't have to be complicated.

I'm a shark. She's chum.

Nature has to take its course, that's just how it is.

"It's been fun, Calder. Thank you. For everything." She

pulls the hotel door open and the hall light stings my vision until I look away. "Really hope we can do this again before you leave ..."

I offer a tight smile, though I'm sure my true sentiments are etched on my face. I've never been good at bluffing when it comes to these moments.

"I'm heading back to the city," I say. "Probably won't see you again."

And by "probably" I mean "definitely."

Hannah's on the other side of the threshold now, clutching her bag under one arm, her hands clasped in front of her like she's about to take communion.

"You don't even know my name, do you?" she asks, not making eye contact.

"I really need to hit the shower, so ..."

"It's Grace," she says. "Not that you care. I just think, you know, we spent the night together. The least you could do is know my name, even if you have no intentions of seeing me again."

I try not to laugh at myself. I was way off.

Where the hell did I get Hannah from?

God, I miss New York girls right now. They don't pull this clingy shit. They don't take a one-night stand to mark the beginnings of a budding relationship. They go their own way in the morning and when you bump into them around town, they pretend like they don't remember you and you pretend like you don't know them and everything's peachy-fucking-keen as life goes on.

"You do this a lot, don't you?" she asks, her light eyes moving onto mine. Grace-not-Hannah tucks a strand of messy blonde sex hair behind one ear.

I lean against the door jamb. "Clearly we had different expectations for ... last night."

Why would she think it was anything other than a run of the mill one-night stand?

"You just ... you seemed different." She worries the inside of her full bottom lip. "Guess I just didn't think I'd feel so ... used."

Oh, god.

"I didn't use you, Grace," I say. "I had a great fucking time with a beautiful blonde I met in a Telluride hotel. I'll never forget it, either. Promise."

She blows a succinct breath between her pink lips. "Until the next blonde in the next hotel."

"Actually, I prefer brunettes, but that's beside the point." I chuckle. She doesn't. "Take care, Grace. All right?"

I step away, gently closing the door, but she stops it with her palm.

"I feel sorry for you." Her eyes are almost a darker shade of blue than they were a second ago. "One of these days, you're going to meet someone amazing, someone who makes you forget all the things you've always wanted to forget. And I hope she breaks your heart."

With that, Grace-not-Hannah pulls her palm from the door and lets it slam.

I hit the shower.

She can curse me all she wants, but you can't get your heart broken if you don't have one.

Chapter 3

Aerin

"Thanks for letting me stay here." I rise on my toes, wrapping my arms around my brother's scrub-covered shoulders despite the fact that he just got home from working an overnight shift in the ER. He's probably covered in a hundred thousand germs and microbes, but I haven't seen him in eight months so I'm too excited to care. "Love the new place."

I pull myself away from Rush and glance out the generous living room windows that offer him a partially-obstructed view of the Brooklyn bridge. He only recently finished his residency and he's not rolling in the dough quite yet, but as a young ER physician, he does well for himself.

"I'm surprised you have a two-bedroom," I say.

"Was going to do the whole roommate thing, but he decided to do the whole Doctors-Without-Borders thing at the last minute." Rush kicks off his tennis shoes and sits his keys down on a table by the door. He looks older than the last time I saw him, naturally, but in a more refined sort of way. There's a different air about him, but I can't quite put my finger on it.

I guess it's hard for me to think of my brother and not picture the scrawny teenager who used to pour my cereal and walk me to the kindergarten bus every morning.

"So who are you working for in the city? You never said." He pulls a pen from his pocket—purple-bodied with some drug logo on the side—and places it beside his keys.

"Oh, um." I don't want to go over specifics with him. For starters, he won't believe me. And if he does, he's going to spend the next thirty minutes lecturing me on what a bad idea this was. Rush makes my pragmatic tendencies look like child's play.

We are what happens when two hippies who don't believe in organized anything (including school) get together and reproduce. If it wasn't for Rush, I don't know that I'd have graduated from high school, and I certainly wouldn't have attended college. Even though he's ten years my senior, he was always more of a father figure than an older brother.

My parents once tried to unenroll me from fifth grade so we could travel the country in an RV. They argued that I'd learn more doing that than I could ever learn sitting in a "boring classroom" all day. They only backed off because they couldn't get financing on the RV they wanted (lack of a job will do that) and Rush threatened to call DHS on them.

"Just some executive," I say. "Owns some technology company in the city. Pretty boring stuff ..."

I hold my breath and cross my fingers that my answer satisfies his curiosity.

"Cool, cool. Well, I'd love to catch up, but I've got to get some sleep," Rush says, squeezing past me. "Going in again tonight for another twelve hours."

"I'm here for a month. We'll have plenty of time to catch up." I offer a tired smile of my own. I had to take a red-eye from LA to NYC since Mr. Welles wanted me to start "as soon as humanly possible."

"Guest bath should be stocked. You might want to get some groceries. Fridge is pretty bare bones right now. There's a number on the fridge for a place that delivers." Rush yawns, his dark eyes squinting as he runs his hands through his even darker hair.

He's always reminded me of Ashton Kutcher, only less goofy and more serious. Like an Ashton-playing-Steve Jobs-and-not-Kelso kind of serious.

Rush would be the ultimate catch for some lucky gal,

and I'm not just saying that because I'm biased. He's ridiculously intelligent, driven, and one of the most selfless people I've ever known.

But he's married to his job. And he's not the cheating type.

We're the same like that, he and I.

Both workaholics, both obsessed with our careers.

Melrose, one of my best friends back in LA, once theorized that since we grew up with such a chaotic home life, our education and careers have been the only thing we've ever been able to control.

And I have to agree.

Relationships will always be shaky ground for us, a great unknown that we couldn't control if we wanted to.

Wheeling my suitcase to the guest suite, I close the door behind me and change out of my travel clothes so I can hit the shower. I always feel so dirty after flying, and a soak in the pristine white tub in the guest bath sounds amazing.

That's another thing about us Keanes. We're clean freaks. Likely another symptom of our misguided parents who didn't believe in cleaning too often because "the chemicals cause cancer."

Ironically enough, our father *almost* died of lung cancer five years ago, and to me, that goes to show you that you can believe anything you want to believe, but at the end of the day life still happens—and if I'm being completely honest, that terrifies me.

I peel out of my clothes and run a steamy bath, unpacking and arranging my toiletries and cosmetics in proper order.

AM skincare.

Makeup.

PM skincare.

Face masks and supplements.

I skim my fingers across the top of the bath water to check the temp before twisting the faucet knobs and stepping inside.

Once submerged, the hot water bakes my skin and the steam fills my lungs. My breaths are shallower than normal and there's a hint of tightness in my chest, which tells me I'm getting anxious.

This always happens before I start a new job. I just want everything to go well. Better than well, actually. Perfect.

Today, I'll try my best to settle in and relax. Tomorrow I'm to report at ten AM to WellesTech headquarters uptown.

I slink down in the water, my back sliding against the white acrylic, and with eyes closed I attempt to pull in the deepest, hardest, fullest breath I can muster.

I can do this.

I can do anything—even things that, to the core of my being, feel like a bad idea.

AVAILABLE NOW!

ACKNOWLEDGMENTS

This book would not have been possible if it weren't for the help of the following amazing individuals. In no particular order ...

Louisa, thank you for another knockout of a cover! And thank you for being so patient and accommodating as always. Alyssa, thank you for working your format magic on my books with my impossible deadlines. Ashley, thank you for beta'ing as always. I couldn't do this without you, and I love your brutal honesty to the moon and back. Christine, Kris, Stacey, Elizette, and Stephanie – thank you for volunteering to do some additional beta reading for me at the last minute! Your feedback was invaluable. Katrina, Chuck, and Max ... always. Wendy, thank you for being so flexible! You're a dream to work with, as always. Neda and the gang at Ardent Prose, thank you for ALL the behind-the-scenes stuff you do. Your service is invaluable and you are a joy to work with! Last, but not least, thank you to all the readers and book bloggers, whether you're a longtime loyalist or reading me for the first time. It's because of you that I get to live my dream, and I'm forever grateful for that.

Reckless

Priceless

The Montgomery Brothers Duet: Dark Paradise

Dark Promises

The P.S. Series

P.S. I Hate You

P.S. I Miss You

P.S. I Dare You

Standalones

Vegas Baby

Cold Hearted

The Perfect Illusion

Country Nights

Absinthe

The Rebound

War and Love

ABOUT THE AUTHOR

Wall Street Journal and #1 Amazon bestselling author Winter Renshaw is a bona fide daydream believer. She lives somewhere in the middle of the USA and can rarely be seen without her trusty Mead notebook and ultra-portable laptop. When she's not writing, she's living the American Dream with her husband, three kids, the laziest puggle this side of the Mississippi, and a busy pug pup that officially owes her three pairs of shoes, one lamp cord, and an office chair (don't ask).

Winter also writes psychological suspense under the name Minka Kent. Her debut novel, THE MEMORY WATCHER, was optioned by NBC Universal in January 2018.

Winter is represented by Jill Marsal of Marsal Lyon Literary Agency.

Like Winter on Facebook.
    Join the private mailing list.

Join Winter's Facebook reader group/discussion group/street team, CAMP WINTER.